POPPYCOCK TALES

By the same author

The Right Way to Read Music (with Michael Baxter)

Berlin Etude

The Soldier and the Orderly Boys

Slopers' Island

POPPYCOCK TALES

Harry F. Baxter

The Book Guild Ltd
Sussex, England

First published in Great Britain in 2005 by
The Book Guild Ltd
25 High Street
Lewes, East Sussex
BN7 2LU

Typesetting in Souvenir Light by
Keyboard Services, Luton, Bedfordshire

Printed in Great Britain by
CPI Bath

A catalogue record for this book is available from
The British Library

ISBN 1 85776 884 1

Contents

List of most characters together with help at pronunciations

DOWMEN von POPO-LOCK	Mayor of Poppycock	as written
HUMPER	largest feet	as written
KRIBBLE-KRABBLE	Joiner	as written
FREETHORF	Undertaker	as written
UNTERSCHNELL	Doctor	Oonter-shnell
DICKKOPF	Stupid chap	Dick-Kopff
BLOOMEN	Florist	as written
SCHMERZ	Dentist	Sh-mare-tz
KNIPER	Inn Keeper	Letter i as in knife
KAHL	Bald Beadle	Carl
RAFFINIERT	Captain of boat	Raff-in-ee-ert
OILER	The owl	as written
GELDMAN	Treasurer	as written – hard G
KÄMPFER	Bull	Kemp-fir
FEIGLING	Young bull	Fi-(as in fire)-gling
GEIZIG	Pork Butcher	Gi-(first i as in fire)-tzish
WEICH	Farm Hand	Vish (i as in fire)
TODTBREW	Poison	Tote-broo
The King		
The Queen		
LEO	the lion	as written
SHEEBA	lioness	as written
TEERLEBER	Circus owner	Tear-labour
GICHT	Councillor	as written (hard G)
MAHOUT	Elephant driver	Mar-hoot
KLUGER	School for brainy	Klooger (hard G)
PACHYDERM	Packy the elephant	Packy-derm
SHWÄTZER	Reverend	Ssh-v-etzer
Mayor's wife		
AGATHODIM	Truth God	Agger-tho-dim
LESERSCHREIBE	A reporter	Lazer-shrie-ba
The Goose		
The Pigeon		
The Cat		

The Mayor and the Seven Men of Poppycock

There was once a town where lived the silliest people in the whole Kingdom of Waxindioren. This was because the cleverest people liked to live in the North, which was cooler. So, the little town attracted only very simple souls and became known, and even famous, for the silliness of its people.

The Mayor settled all disputes and he was very proud of his reputation as the main citizen of the very little town of Poppycock. No matter what the problem, Mayor Dowmen von Popo-lock always knew how best to help so that everyone was satisfied. And many are the true stories of his cleverness. I really should tell you about some of the problems he solved.

One day, while out for a walk with his peacock, Popo, as everyone called the Mayor for short, saw below him, in a field where seven cows grazed, seven men he knew to be good people of Poppycock. As he watched, Fowen, the peacock, cried out and showed his colours, which told the Mayor that great problems were to be solved down below in the field where the cows chewed the grass. One of the cows looked up and mooed a welcome to the peacock. This was a sure sign that the cow had been listening to the seven men of Poppycock and knew the answer to their problem.

1

So, now I must tell you a secret. But, first you must promise never to tell anyone, because the Mayor of Poppycock would certainly be very upset if he learned that I had told you the secret of his success.

When the Mayor was a little boy, his mother – who was the prettiest lady in the whole of Poppycockland but had six fingers on her left hand – had taught her son always to listen to the animals, who understand all human problems and can always think of a good way to help.

So the Mayor walked down the hill and into the field where the seven little men of Poppycock counted each other but always came to six as the answer.

'Oh, Mayor Dowmen von Popo-lock, it is good you are here. We were seven when we left home but now we are only six. We promised our wives never to leave one of us behind because of the terrible dragon.'

Now, I must tell you that, for a whole year, the people of Poppycock had been tormented by a fierce dragon which lived ... well, truly no-one knew exactly where, but it frightened all the people, who had never actually seen it but had heard it and knew for sure that it meant to eat them one day.

The Mayor looked around him and felt sad that it really did seem they had lost one of their number for, as he watched, he saw old Humper – who lived in a cottage on the hill called Buckeldoin and who was thought to be the wisest labourer in the neighbourhood because he had the largest feet and could not be knocked over when the men played the 'Pushing Game' – count out aloud.

'One, two, three, four, five, six.' It was correct: there was a man there who was missing, thought the Mayor.

'Let's do another count,' said the Mayor, while he

2

thought how to ask the cow so that the others should not see where the knowledge was gained.

So Kribble-Krabble, the Joiner, stepped forward and counted the rest of the men: but he still could make it only six: and that was as well because his schoolmaster had never thought it necessary to teach further than six for who, except a banker, wanted to trouble his head with high financial matters? And Kribble-Krabble stood back among his friends, who now looked to the Mayor to solve the mystery.

Everybody felt cross with Kribble-Krabble, for it is always so, that people who are worried try to blame someone else so that they should not feel themselves so guilty. And Kribble-Krabble was so annoying: he scratched himself all his waking hours, but more than ever when he became upset.

'Turn your backs while I think how to solve this problem,' said the Mayor pompously.

The peacock looked at the cow with an amused grin. Of course, every child knows that animals can talk to each other without actually speaking words. I cannot think why adults do not all know this for, if they did, they would be a lot more careful about what they say in front of their pets. Anyway, if you had been there you would have known what the peacock said to the cow and have laughed out loud and maybe upset the Mayor.

So, all the seven men of Poppycock obediently turned round while the Mayor quickly moved over and put his ear to the cow, who told him what to do. A big smile came over the Mayor's face, for now he knew how to solve the riddle.

'You may all turn round now,' he said, feeling full of

his own importance. And, while the cow politely stepped aside, the Mayor pointed to a pat the cow had conveniently prepared for the ceremony.

'Each man must make his mark with his nose on the cowpat,' said the Mayor. 'Then, if everyone does this properly, we shall know which one of you is missing.' And the Mayor watched while everyone put his nose into the cowpat and so left behind a nose mark.

'One, two, three, four, five, six, seven,' counted old Humper with great accuracy. And the peacock knew the cow was laughing as she strolled away to tell her husband, the bull, about the silliness of the seven men of the little town of Poppycock.

So, once again, the people of Poppycock rejoiced at their cleverness in having chosen as Mayor such a clever fellow as the very noble Dowmen von Popo-lock, about whom tales were fast spreading well outside his Mayordom.

The Little Boat

The Town Hall of Poppycock was all gilt and dignity.
There was Mr Kribble-Krabble dressed in his best suit,
and Mr Humper wearing his Sunday boots which squeaked
at every step though they were twenty years old. Twenty
squeaky steps he took along the Council Chamber before
taking his place beside Mr Freethorf, the Undertaker
who, to make his face longer and more suitable for his
job, exercised the muscles of his chin every day before
he got out of bed. One morning, soon after their marriage,
Mrs Freethorf had called Doctor Unterschnell, whose
diagnoses were famous and who had, while Mr Freethorf
was still finishing the first fifty face contortions, decided
that Mr Freethorf was suffering from epilepsy: but that
is quite another story. I expect you know all about it, for
it was very well reported in the *Poppycock Daily Crier*.

Just then Mayor Dowmen von Popo-lock looked through
the spy-hole bored through the big picture painted on
the wall, which looked into the next room – the Council
Chamber. I should tell you about this hole, for the story
of it has been kept secret for much too long. But, here
and now, I can tell you only the bare facts or you will
forget about the Councillors who are waiting next door,
and that has been done too often in the past for me to
want to do it here. Anyway, you can see that the

gentleman whose breeches are splitting is the one who, for all these years, has so kindly accommodated successive Mayors of Poppycock and allowed them to keep abreast of things.

'They're not all here yet,' said the Mayor, getting down from the chair he had used to peer through the hole and lying down again on the couch placed in the Mayor's parlour. There is a very funny story about that couch, but I think I had better not tell it now or you will laugh so much that you will be put off the story of the little boat.

Anyway, almost as soon as the Mayor lay down the others came into the Chamber next door. There was Mr DickKopf, whose suggestions were nearly always so terribly stupid and who never grasped what was being debated at the meetings; then there was Mr Bloomen, who grew very beautiful flowers and sold them in his shop by the harbour; there was Mr Kniper, who owned the Inn where it was said smugglers used to gather in the old days; and, lastly, Mr Schmerz, the Dentist of Poppycock. Oh, I nearly forgot to tell you that Doctor Unterschnell always attended Council meetings, just to deal with any Councillor who fainted from the strain – for you cannot have Councillors falling about all over the place, can you?

The Beadle, who was not a breed of dog but a Mr Kahl, who had not a single hair upon his head, called out to the Mayor that everyone was present and that the meeting could begin. Mr Kahl was proud of his head, for it made him different. It was his shining glory. He held the gold chain while the Mayor struggled into it and, with this authority, they went together into the Council Chamber. Everybody rose to their feet and the Mayor

7

took his seat at the head of the long rosewood table around which all the Councillors were seated.

'We are here, at this Extraordinary Meeting, to discuss a very extraordinary matter,' said the Mayor. 'There has been no sign of growth, whatever, and it is my opinion that action is needed or we shall lose our little boat, which will never last through the winter.'

Now I must tell you that the good people of Poppycock had long wanted a boat to save them the troublesome journey right around the bay every time they wanted to leave their town and visit the other side. They had saved up and planned to buy a boat big enough to take fifty people each trip. On the day decided they had turned out almost to a man and all the population had been there to see the Captain of the ship bring the vessel for their inspection into the harbour from across the narrow strait.

Captain Raffiniert had heard of these simple people but, in all his life, he had never been so astonished at what happened next. Instead of examining his ship – the one he had brought to sell to them – the good people assembled had gasped and stared lovingly at the little rowing boat tied astern. He had looked and listened. Soon it became evident that there would be no sale of the ship and no profit as he had expected.

'Oh, how pretty,' they had shouted, lifting their children above their heads to give the little ones a better view. 'See how it follows its mother.' The Captain stared at his little rowing boat – seeing it for the first time with different eyes. He realised as he watched that these people were not joking.

Well, I expect you have guessed already what happened?

The whole population had been charmed by the sight of the little boat which never left its mother's side. The Captain did not tell them, of course, that the little boat was attached by a thin rope which could not be seen because it was mostly under water, and the good people of Poppycock were not looking for what they had not thought about. After a hurried consultation the good Mayor Dowmen von Popo-lock had sent for the Captain to come off his bridge and hear their decision.

'It has all the virtues, but none of the drawbacks,' said the Mayor. 'It is young enough to learn to do exactly what we want it to do and' (and here the Mayor had paused and gazed fondly at the little boat) 'it is much cheaper.'

The Captain knew not what to say. He did know, however, that if he did not sell them the little rowing boat he was likely not to make a sale at all – so set had they all now become on having a 'baby boat'. The problem was what to say in answer to their question 'How long will it take to be fully grown?' Finally he sold them the little boat without actually giving an answer to this question. And how happily the men of Poppycock carried home their prize.

They nearly fell over each other showing off the baby boat to the few citizens who had stayed at home in Poppycock. 'We paid so little for it, and look how sweet it is. Besides, it will grow up and be just as big as its mother – and think of the saving.' Everyone was truly happy, for they all could see for themselves what a bargain had been obtained.

The next few weeks were very happy and exciting for all the people of Poppycock. Of course, there were problems. You would expect that, for whoever before had brought up a baby boat without its mother? What did baby boats eat? This is where Doctor Unterschnell helped. He remembered from his student days that baby boats thrived on hay. So the finest hay was collected and the farms around were proud to contribute to feed the, by now, famous little boat. Not only did the population of Poppycock daily visit the little boat but people came from many miles around. After a week the Mayor told the Council that the town would have to charge a small fee to outsiders because they were using the town's amenities. One day they had drunk nearly all the water of the town's supply – and so must help pay for the extra work so many visitors caused. Of course, if the Council were to charge visitors it did seem fair that the citizens should also charge a little extra for this and that – just to help, you understand? So the little Town of Poppycock actually made a good deal of money because the good and wise Mayor, Dowmen von Popo-lock, had seen fit to choose the little baby boat instead of the great big grown-up parent costing a thousand times as much. Of course, there were those who remembered that the Mayor alone had opposed the purchase of the ship.

From the very beginning he had said that the town could not afford such a large expense. There were others who wondered whether the Mayor had, from the beginning, planned to buy the baby boat just to make money for the town and its people. But these people quickly agreed in their minds that, whether the Mayor had planned it or not, what was happening was interesting, exciting and very profitable.

10

However, the little boat had not grown and the people were growing impatient. The Doctor's reputation was at stake. The Town Clerk's pride was at stake. Even the honour of the town was at stake for, believing the words of the Mayor, all the population from the dignitaries down to the humblest peasant had acted, among themselves and with all the many visitors, as though the little boat could not fail to develop into a big ship because of the good attention they lavished on it at all times. Concern turned to doubt, and this led to trouble for, already, visitors were to be seen standing pointing at the dear little boat and laughing out loud and clear. This was when the Town Clerk had gone to see the priest, who had blessed the little boat and all those who were to sail in her. Together they had gone to see the Doctor, who had just come from treating a ewe who had quite positively refused to tell him what was wrong with her but had told the good Doctor more frankly than ever did his human patients that he was a fool to believe that all was well with the little boat.

The good Mayor, Dowmen von Popo-lock, had merely smiled and called an Extraordinary Meeting of the Council to deal with the problem.

'What is your opinion of what to do?' the Mayor asked of Mr Kniper.

Mr Kniper gazed around, his dull expression making it evident that he was not used to being asked an opinion.

'Well you, Councillor Schmerz?'

The good Dentist stopped playing with his navel, which he could reach through the opening in his shirt. He looked simply astonished that such a lordly person as the Mayor should need to ask a mere dentist.

'All right, you,' said the Mayor, pointing his mace at the undertaker.

'Me?' stammered Councillor Freethorf. 'I can only suggest we bury it and see if that will help it grow.'

'Idiot,' said the Doctor, under his breath.

'Imbecile,' said the Beadle quietly, though he was supposed to remain impartial.

'Well you, good Councillor Unterschnell,' said the Mayor, leaning forward and staring the Doctor in the eyes. 'You are a man of learning. Tell us. What is wrong with our boat that it does not grow big and strong like its mother?'

The Doctor had no more idea than that man whose face you can see any cold night if you stare long enough at the moon.

'Well,' he said, his mind racing to find something credible to say, 'It never has eaten its hay, and has refused all other food.' This was fact, but it gave the Doctor his sought-after answer. 'It's undernourished,' he said triumphantly.

There was an undercurrent of feeling against the Doctor. He who had been so full of how well he knew how to feed baby boats; he in whom everybody placed so much faith. The poor fellow knew his explanation was unacceptable. He sank back into the hugeness of his Council chair.

'I know what to do,' said a voice everyone remembered as having uttered more stupidities than any other three Councillors put together. 'Tell the people that the little boat has typhus and then burn it for all to see.'

Everyone stared at Councillor DickKopf. There seemed nothing more to say after hearing such idiotic profanity.

12

Yet, slowly, they began to see some sense in such a solution.

'No!' said the Mayor loudly. 'I have given the matter the benefit of my great experience and now know what is wrong.'

Everyone stared at the Mayor. His voice held the sound of conviction. He let his gaze go from face to face. The admiration he could see in their eyes was no more than he had expected. Suddenly he rose to his feet and, with an imperious hand-beckon for the others to follow, stalked out of the Chamber towards a destination not declared. The Councillors looked astonished but followed in twos and threes, and a goodly sight they made as, in their Councillor's robes, they all trailed after the Mayor, who walked with his Beadle and, looking neither to the right nor to the left, was well aware of the interest aroused and of the people who began to follow until quite a crowd had assembled and formed into a long queue behind the lordly-looking Dowmen von Popo-lock.

Now I have to tell you that the Mayor had been more than a little worried. After all, he had bought a little boat instead of a steamer large enough to carry fifty people each trip across the strait. He had said it would grow – and why not? Do we not all start out little? Could he not well remember being barely as tall as the bulges on his mother's chest? Yet, later, he had been able to look down at those bulges and, from the height that age had given him, had known for the first time that ladies are much nicer than men. But, unlike himself, the little boat had not grown.

When the people had really become restive and everybody had racked their brains for a reason the Mayor

13

had known he must do something or forever lose the respect he had been so very careful to build into his life and position as the leading citizen of Poppycock. Gradually, as the days had lengthened into weeks, he had become desperate. Why did not the confounded thing grow? Was it just being stubborn?

One night, unable to sleep, he had slipped out and gone quickly to the little boat and asked it to grow.

'Please,' he had begged. 'You must grow. I have promised everyone you will become big and be able to carry fifty passengers as does your mother.' He had looked very silly, there in the moonlight begging favours of the little boat and wearing only his night-cap and the long night-gown tucked under his cloak.

The owl in the nearby tree had laughed so much. 'Be quiet, you silly bird,' the Mayor had whispered menacingly. 'You'll bring someone out to see what all the noise is about.'

Oiler, the owl, had stopped laughing immediately and shocked the Mayor by daring to answer him so insolently.

'Silly, am I?' said the owl. 'Soon the people will demand a new Mayor; one who doesn't waste their money on little boats; a Mayor who knows how to make little boats grow into big ones; a man who keeps his promises.' And the creature had laughed until the Mayor had run away home because people had started to open their windows to learn what all the fuss was about.

'You have made a big mistake in being so rude to Mr Oiler the owl,' said Fowen, the Mayor's peacock, as soon as he heard about his master's escapade. And the Mayor had argued with his peacock, who told him frankly and repeatedly to go back and apologise. The Mayor knew

14

his peacock was right, but it had taken a fortnight and much loss of dignity.

So now the Mayor and the owl had a secret and not one of the admiring crowd who followed the Mayor had the least notion of what was to happen or whose clever idea was being used to solve the problem of the little boat which could not or would not grow.

The procession reached the little boat and the Mayor told the Councillors to pick it up and to follow him – which they did, right down to the wharf. There they stood and listened to the Mayor while he told them of the need to return the little boat to its mother.

'It is homesick,' he explained. 'We took it away from its mother when it was too young.'

A gasp of sympathy went through the crowd. Some of the women cried, and Doctor Unterschnell was not alone among the men to have a tear in his eye – though I must confess I think it was from rage and not compassion. Why had he not thought of that, he asked himself in growing frustration? And a tear certainly fell from the eye of Mr Oiler, the owl, as he stared down at the Mayor's peacock, which had seen the crowd and followed at a safe distance. But, again, I do not think it was caused by emotion, for careful scrutiny would have revealed that the owl and the peacock were crying with laughter.

So, when the good Captain arrived in his steamer, it was perfectly obvious to all the good people of Poppycock that the little boat was quite overjoyed again to be at its mother's side for it slid gently through the water, keeping so very near to her side, until right out of sight. And the Captain immediately agreed to keep the little boat with its mother until nature, in all her wisdom, should bring it to maturity, when it could be used as originally intended by the patient, kind, but rather silly people of the little town of Poppycock who, to this day, still talk about their little boat which did not grow because it was homesick for its mother.

The Two Knights of Poppycock

The King of Waxindioren was very annoyed. The town of Poppycock had not paid the annual tax and still owed nearly two thousand Pengels, which is a great deal of money no matter how one looks at the matter. Mayor Dowmen von Popo-lock was more astonished than worried. How could it be? All the people of Poppycock were such honest fellows, yet the King's tax collectors had been all week examining the accounts and there was no doubt – the money had not been paid.

There was only one thing to do – start from the beginning – so he sent for Mr Geldman, who was the Town Treasurer. Mr Geldman arrived all hot and panting because he had hurried all the way from his house as soon as he had heard what the Mayor's messenger had said.

'You'd best come at once, Mr Geldman. Popo' – for that is what the people affectionately called the Mayor behind his back – 'has received a message from the King.'

Treasurer Geldman thought this could mean only one thing. At last he was to receive proper recognition for his services. A knighthood? An earldom? A dukedom? At last he would equal his wife's family – they who all these years had lorded over him their claim to honour,

17

for his mother-in-law had received the honour in person from the Queen. And, as the Mother Medal had been slipped over her head and the Queen had smiled and shaken hands, the King was heard to whisper in an aside 'Such a small reward for such colossal stupidity' and, hearing this, Geldman's mother-in-law had been prouder than ever of her success in bearing fifteen children. Was it not obvious that the King himself took an interest and thought the reward insufficient for such effort of service to the country?

The Treasurer shuffled his feet, a little annoyed at being kept waiting after having made such an athletic effort to arrive as quickly as possible.

'Ah! The very man,' said Mayor Dowmen von Popolock, entering the room suddenly and before the Treasurer had time to alter his scowl to an expression of abject obedience. 'You are the very man to explain why our tax debt has not been paid.'

There was a silence while the Treasurer thought how best to answer, for you must understand that Mr Geldman was like all those who love money – not really very intelligent and lacking in imagination.

'Come now, said the Mayor, as though talking to a naughty child. 'Why? Why? Why?'

'Because...' and Geldman stopped, not knowing how to say what had to be said.

'Yes?' said the Mayor, demandingly.

'Well, sir... The ... the knights.'

The Mayor seemed puzzled. 'What have my knights to do with it?' The matter was plainly boring to the Mayor. Suddenly his expression changed to one of understanding and he bent close to the now cringing Treasurer. 'Are

19

you saying that we have not paid our taxes because of my knights?'

'They cost fifteen hundred Pengels, plus cartage,' stammered Mr Geldman, relieved that the lordly Mayor Dowmen von Popo-lock at last had been told.

And that is why the revered, lordly, magnificent Dowmen von Popo-lock, Mayor and first citizen of Poppycock, was summoned to the palace to see the King of Waxindioren and to explain why he had not seen to it that the annual tax was paid.

Now I must tell you that you need have no fears – absolutely not. Our undefeatable and intrepid Mayor of Poppycock went to the palace, not as an abject debtor owing money he could not pay but as the first citizen of a wonderful people, though they were few in number and held to be silly, in the Kingdom of Waxindioren. His lordly and aristocratic bearing impressed the Queen, and the King found it quite impossible to intimidate a man whose self-assurance was no less than his own – yet whose knowledge of etiquette was quite astonishing – after expecting a badly dressed country bumpkin to appear all apologetic and confused. But that visit deserves a story on its own. I shall probably tell it to you later but, for now, let me tell you that, though Mayor Dowmen von Popo-lock had been such a success, he still left the Palace with the words of the King's Treasurer ringing in his ears.

'We expect the money in full not an hour later than the first day of Masselmick,' which everybody knows is one day before Metonic, and gave the Mayor two whole months in which to report back with the money.

As soon as the Mayor's party had reached a safe

twenty leagues out of sight of the palace on the way home the Mayor called a halt while he performed his pabulatums. Now I must tell you that one of the Mayor's secrets was that, whenever he had been put under strain, he would find somewhere quite alone and relieve his nerves by voluntary shaking of his body, pulling faces, and any other movements normally not made but through which a nervous state can disintegrate. These contortions he called his pabulatums and, though he believed faithfully that no one knew, the acts had been seen, understood and accepted by those around him and all of Poppycock knew that the Mayor had fits which helped him to solve all the many problems. There are many stories about the Mayor's pabulatums but I must tell you them some other time. Right now I can tell you only that he walked off to a field distant from the camp which his party were putting up for the night and there began his most severe facial and body pabulatums.

Oblivious to the many eyes watching he grimaced and grunted, and waggled and wiggled, and cackled and cried, and hollered and hooted, and twisted and turned – and all the while the watchful eyes grew bigger and their owners leaned ever nearer so as not to miss a single detail of such a once-in-a-lifetime spectacle. Suddenly one of the baby foxes fell off the steep bank and rolled down to the Mayor's dancing feet. Instantly its mother – who never would have shown herself except to save her little son – sprang down and picked up the little fox.

The Mayor, startled out of his wits, stared at the harmless pair, who stared back, not knowing what else to do.

'You've been watching me,' gasped the Mayor, panting

from his exertions. 'I'll have you put in the stocks for that.'

'Don't be silly,' said the mother fox, whose name was Vixen. 'My feet are much too dainty and I have four. Besides, it's not a crime to watch a human enjoy a dance.'

'A dance?' said the Mayor indignantly. 'I wasn't dancing. These are my pabulatums.'

'Then you must teach me how to do them,' said Vixen, 'for we know only the fox-trot!'

And, little by little, the Mayor, who never could resist a good talk and knew the value of learning from animals, told his troubles to the foxes who, seeing Vixen and her son so well in conversation with the human being in the hollow, all came out to inspect this strange creature who looked so like other humans but acted so differently and could speak so that they understood.

'But, my dear Mayor,' said the leader of the foxes. 'You have no problem. All you have to do...' and the Mayor's eyes grew brighter and the smile on his face grew ever bigger as he listened to the cleverest, most cunning solution to all his difficulties.

And so it was that His Grace, Dowmen von Popolock, Mayor of Poppycock in the Kingdom of Waxindioren, once again listened attentively while a non-human creature poured out wisdom to solve a problem only humans can make so serious.

The Mayor said goodbye to the foxes, thanking their leader sincerely for the wonderful suggestions which the Mayor felt in his bones would work.

'Glad to have been of help,' said the fox leader. 'Besides, we have enjoyed your dancing. It gave us much

22

pleasure.' And I must tell you that, if you ever go past that place in your wanderings, you could well see the foxes of Waxindioren doing their dances, which are wild and always done standing on their two back legs. It has come down through the generations, you see, and marvellous it is to behold. But do not expect everybody to be able to see them for only those who most truly love all animals can be allowed to see such a wonderful imitation of the merry pabulatums of the great Popo.

Back in Poppycockland Mayor Dowmen von Popolock lost no time in following the advice of the fox.

Now I could tell you a secret, but you can guess it for yourself for, if you had been watching the Mayor's house, you would have seen old Humper arrive and go round to the back door where the Mayor let him in. And then, if you had peeped inside the Mayor's study, you would have seen the Mayor put on a black helmet and then a white one, as if to decide which was the better. A few minutes later you would have seen old Humper put both helmets under his cloak and you would have had to move smartly to avoid being seen, because Humper moved very quickly when he had an important errand to do. This was so now, for he shuffled with great speed out of the house and towards the main gate of the little town.

Now the Mayor had a beautiful picture book which had been his mother's and in it was a coloured picture of a town in Himmelland. The gateway to this wonderful town was tall and on it, on either side, was a knight on horseback. And, for many years, the Mayor had wanted to have such figures on the imposing entrance to Poppycock.

23

By now you will have guessed correctly where the money for the annual tax had gone! Yes – you are absolutely right. The Mayor had used it to pay the masons who had been called from the neighbouring town of Steinmauer, because they were the best builders of such things in the whole Kingdom of Waxindioren. And everybody had been glad that the Mayor had caused the knights to be built, for they sat there on their horses and looked so imposing.

And, now that the Mayor had taken the advice given him by the foxes, it was said by everyone that, at midnight on some nights, the two knights changed places. Did you ever hear such nonsense? Yet it was a fact that the knight with the black helmet had been on the left but, that night, he had come down from his horse and changed over with the knight on the right. You could easily know this for certain because one knight had a black helmet and the other a white one. It was astonishing, but wonderful. And, gradually, people began to come from other towns to see the knights. Crowds would gather at the weekends and at holiday times and there was much excitement as, nearing midnight, they peered into the darkness and tried to see the miraculous change take place. Once there was a cry from someone in the crowd that he had actually seen the knights run along the parapet from horse to horse.

'They shook hands as they passed each other,' he cried. 'I saw them!'

And old Humper, who had just a few seconds later come on the scene, smiled to himself and congratulated the man on such good fortune.

'It is a good omen for they come to life only for a

second or two, and only special people can see them alive,' he declared, shaking the excited man by the hand.

And it was not long before the Mayor announced that a charge would have to be made for all visitors who wanted to stay up and watch for the change of the knights. So the Town Crier rang his bell at five minutes to midnight and then made a collection of a Pengel for men and half a Pengel for ladies; and many a gentleman was pleased to invite his lady or somebody else's lady to stand with him in the dark and keep a sharp look-out for the change of the knights. And very enjoyable nights they were too!

So you will not be surprised to learn that the good Mayor Dowmen von Popo-lock was able to return to the palace and not only pay the annual tax for two years but take a most beautiful present for the Queen as well. But that is another story. I must just tell you that, on his way to the palace, the good Mayor, who never forgot his friends, stopped off in a certain hollow and that there was a party like you never did see – for the foxes had been practising their pabulatums and the Mayor gave them the best display of his life, even though he had no nervous tension but only happiness in his system.

The Pugnacious Bull

Mr Kämpfer was a bull. He had been very strong when he was born but, now that he was two years old – which is about twenty in human years – he was certainly the strongest living creature in the whole Kingdom of Waxindioren. Did I ever tell you how it came to have such an outlandish name? No? Well, I shall ... but not now, for I must get on with my telling you about Mr Kämpfer, the strongest bull in the world.

I should tell you that Mr Kämpfer had begun to fight as soon as he was born. He tossed the master's black bitch, Ping-a-Pong, because she came over to investigate him. He stood on his four little feet and bellowed loudly to let the world know his superiority. It was not long before even his own mother said he was a nuisance and needed a thrashing. The trouble was that no one could be found capable of thrashing the young bull. Only Kämpfer's father could have done this, but he had gone the way of all troublesome bulls and was not available to chastise his son.

Not everybody hated Mr Kämpfer. You know, do you not, that a bull is the man and a cow is a lady bull? Well, Mr Kämpfer soon grew to be so strong, so fierce, so powerful and so handsome that all the lady bulls wanted his favours. The other bulls hated him, but every one was afraid of him, for they knew what happened to bulls who dared to challenge the great Kämpfer. And then one day he tossed the farm manager, who had hit him with a stick. This is where our good friend Mayor Dowmen von Popo-lock comes into the story.

Walking along a footpath in a field one fine evening the good Mayor heard sobbing that made the world indeed a miserable-sounding place. It was a young cow who cried noisily and messily into the ground and so caused mushrooms to grow there early the next morning. And if you have ever heard cows cry you will know that the sound, to human ears, is like a cross between an overheated locomotive and an unoiled farmyard gate.

Now you must already know that good Mayor Dowmen von Popo-lock is really a very kind man.

'What on earth is the matter that you make such a hullabaloo?' he asked. And the cow stopped her crying and stared at this human-looking creature who could speak so that she could so clearly understand.

'They've taken him away,' said the cow, shaking huge tears from her eyelashes.

As the Mayor stood there he had not the least idea of what the cow meant and, certainly, he had no idea who had been taken away. He intended to pat the cow on the head, give her a peppermint and tell her she would grow out of it as soon as she was a little older but, even as he searched in the pocket of his breeches for a peppermint, there came a noise he could only suppose could be two dozen cows, all crying bitterly. And so it was for, hearing voices, the herd had joined their sister who was crying to the Mayor and all began to cry afresh.

So the story was told. The lordly Mayor Dowmen von Popo-lock sat down on a toadstool while he heard tales of the magnificent, beautiful, powerful, loveable, adorable, masterly, handsome bull they all called Mr Kämpfer. Each one had a different tale to tell. Each one seemed, without jealousy, to love the absent Mr Kämpfer and to want him back among them. As the darkness descended the Mayor heard how Mr Kämpfer had thrashed the bully of a neighbouring herd; how he had kept order and dominated – truly a King among animals. No one had dared to cross his path and even the humans had feared but admired him, for the Mayor learned how proud the herdsman had been of looking after this, the most fearsome bull he had ever known. People came from far away just to see Mr Kämpfer – to stand and look at him. As the Mayor listened a great desire grew ever stronger in him to see this paragon of bovine perfection.

'So you must help,' said Daisy, who had that name because she ate them as fast as she could scoop them into her big, generous mouth.

'But, how can I do that?' asked the Mayor, by now feeling not only a great sympathy for all the sad cows but also a strong interest to see for himself the most magnificent bull in the world. 'I don't even know where he is ... where they have taken your ... your...'

'I'll tell you where he's gone,' said a voice from the darkness. The cows immediately shouted back and told the bull, who was with a lot of other young bulls on the other side of the fence, to shut up and be quiet.

'Wait!' said the Mayor. 'Let us hear where Mr Kämpfer is supposed to have gone.'

So the cows were silent and the bull on the other side

29

of the fence, and whose name was Mr Feigling, told them how glad he and his brethren were that Mr Kämpfer had tossed the farm manager because that had sealed his fate and was why Mr Kämpfer was now waiting to be made into a great big beef sausage, so that he could cause no more trouble.

At this the cows began such a pitiable crying that, before he could think what he was doing, the Mayor sprang to his feet shouting 'He shall not be a sausage!' This caused instant, astonished silence. How wonderful to have such a gallant Mayor! Even the bulls – who, of course, hated beef sausages – were delighted at a human who could feel so strongly against beef sausages.

The Mayor strode to the fence and faced the bulls. 'You stupid creatures. Can't you see? You have to have a leader. There has always to be a leader: and' – the Mayor waved his arm around to show all the cows in the moonlight – 'there's enough lady bulls here, one for every one of you. I'm sure Mr Kämpfer didn't want them all.' The bulls clustered around the fence and peered at all the lady bulls on the other side. 'Now!' said the Mayor. 'Where have they taken your leader; your King Bull?'

'He'll make the beautifullest, biggest, best beef sausage ever seen!' shouted Mr Feigling.

'He'll make minced beef of you when he comes back,' said the Mayor, though he had never seen Mr Kämpfer. And the other bulls grunted their little short grunts, which told the cows and the Mayor that they were thinking now of two things. One was that it was true that if Mr Kämpfer returned he would quickly but severely sort out those who had spoken against him. The second thought was what the Mayor had said - 'You've got to have a leader – your King Bull.' It was nice, somehow, put like that, to think of themselves as a herd under a really positive King Bull. Suddenly the loss of Mr Kämpfer seemed a tragedy and, slowly and one by one, they began to chant.

'We want Mr Kämpfer! We want Mr Kämpfer!' they bellowed.

Mayor Dowmen von Popo-lock had heard enough. He raised his arms for silence. 'I will bring Mr Kämpfer back among you,' he said. 'But, first you must all make me a promise.' Every cow and every bull stared at the Mayor. It was a quaint scene – the lordly, imposing, aristocratic member of the human race standing there in the moonlight extracting promises of good behaviour from two herds of cattle, male and female. Suddenly he turned and was gone.

Now I have to tell you that Mr Geizig did make sausages. And one day, while out picking Todtbrew, the flowers of which he boiled to make a food with which he poisoned the local cats, he chanced to see Mr Kämpfer. 'A good herd,' thought Mr Geizig, 'but never, in all my life, have I seen such a bull.'

As he stared at the massive mountain of power in the field Mr Geizig's imagination turned Mr Kämpfer's huge body into an enormous sausage. The thought lived with him after that both night and day. Perhaps he could go down in history as maker of the biggest sausage in the world? And, when Mr Weich's farm manager appeared one evening to say that he had persuaded his employer to sell Mr Kämpfer, it was not long before the gold was taken out of the pot behind the chimney in Mr Geizig's

31

house and put into the breeches' pocket of Mr Weich's farm manager.

'Tossed you, did he?' snarled Mr Geizig. 'By thunder, he won't toss me!'

But that very evening Mr Kämpfer tossed Mr Geizig into the air, caught him as he came down and then stamped on him, with the warning, 'Mad, cruel man. Try to beat me again and I'll squash you as though you were a fly.' But, of course, Mr Geizig would not have understood the bull's warning words even if he had been conscious to hear them.

Very soon all of Poppycock was laughing because, at last, Mr Geizig had met his match – tossed by a bull he was beating with a stick.

The next day the Town Crier had in his news that Mr Geizig was offering one thousand Pengels to any man whose bull could fight and beat Mr Kämpfer. But no bull could be made to enter the ring and face up to the challenge. The first two took one look at Mr Kämpfer and then bolted so fast and so far that they have never been seen again. The next one fainted and fell on top of the good Doctor Unterschnell, who was there to see fair play. Another walked up to Mr Kämpfer and kissed him as a token of utter submission and backed out of the ring, treading on people's toes as he went. And Mr Kämpfer treated each bull in turn with absolute contempt.

The crowd had laughed itself sick but was becoming bored when they brought in the bull terriers. Staffordshires they were, and Mr Kämpfer alerted himself to a new experience, for these dogs were more stupidly brave than any dog he had previously met. He flung fourteen back at their owners before Mayor Popo appeared.

The Mayor bent down and, picking up one of the little Stafford dogs which was bleeding, spoke softly to it while he cradled it in his arms.

They had never seen their Mayor angry and the crowd stood silent and waited. For I must explain that, in the days long ago, people were not very kind to their animals for life was very much harder than now. So, if the bull tossed their dogs, the owners let the poor creatures lie there injured – for what worth was a dog when beaten and not in perfect health? I must tell you a good story about these little bull terriers, but just now I must go on with the tale of Mr Kämpfer.

Just as Mayor Dowmen von Popo-lock could somehow give out a friendship to animals before they had heard him say a word, a sort of very strong feeling that shone from him like an electric current, so he gave out now the feeling of anger. The crowd felt it and it made them all feel guilty.

'He's good for nothing else,' they shouted, pointing at Mr Kämpfer. They just could not suppose that their Mayor was cross about the little dog or any of the other dogs lying about.

'He's the most dangerous animal in the world,' shouted Mr Geizig, his arm in a sling and a bandage on his head.

'Will you give him to me if I can lead him away quietly?' asked the Mayor, walking towards Mr Kämpfer.

The Mayor's Beadle stepped bravely into the ring beside his master. 'It is my duty to protect you,' he said. 'I cannot allow you near such danger.' The Mayor gently put the injured dog in the Beadle's arms and told him to care for it properly. Just then Mrs Weich stepped forward.

'We bred him and he is dangerous,' she said. 'All his life he has fought and terrorised everyone. Even all the other bulls are frightened of him. He tossed our farm manager so we let him go to Mr Geizig, who wants to make a giant sausage of him – the biggest sausage in the world. No man can handle this big bull, and you've seen what he has done with the dogs. He's no good for anything but he'll make a lovely sausage.'

'May I have him if I can lead him away quietly?' repeated the Mayor.

'Yes!' roared the crowd.

'You must not try,' roared the Beadle.

'Let us see you lead him away!' roared the crowd. 'We want to see if you can for, if you can't, nobody can.'

The Mayor stepped up to Mr Geizig. 'What did you pay for him?' he asked, taking out a purse and offering five pieces of gold into the one good hand of the sausage-maker.

Mr Geizig looked at Mr Kämpfer, who was idly watching all these proceedings with a strange calm. A great fear was in the heart of Mr Geizig, a fear he was anxious to hide. If he turned down the gold he would still be the owner of the huge, fierce bull, and all the crowd would wait to see him lead the animal from the ring and into the sausage mill – a feat he knew would show his terror of Mr Kämpfer. Quietly he put the gold into his pocket. 'You can have him,' he said, with a hasty laugh 'if you can lead him away.'

'I will lead him away on one condition,' said the Mayor; and everybody began to be frightened that their Mayor was so serious, for they began to realise that he could be very badly hurt – yet they were all curious to know how the Mayor would deal with the savage bull and they all knew that their Mayor had never failed to succeed in anything he undertook to do.

'What condition?' they all shouted, beside themselves with excitement.

'If I can prove he's docile and quite a nice bull when treated properly, will the good citizen herd-owner, Mr Weich, let him go back to the herd?' asked the Mayor.

Now, Mr Weich was intrigued by the idea that the Mayor should think he could handle Mr Kämpfer. All his life he had bred bulls, but never such a one as the gigantic Mr Kämpfer. Yet, had Mayor Dowmen von Popolock not done many wonderful things and solved problems when the brains of Poppycock were at their wits' end to know what to do? Could he really tame the most unmanageable, most savage bull ever known? Sometimes it seemed that the Mayor could perform magic. Some said he could actually talk with animals of every kind. No! It could not be true - yet, how were they to know if he was not given the chance to try? And, if he were to succeed why, then Mr Kämpfer was the best bull he had ever seen.

'Done!' he cried out. 'If you can lead him away peacefully ... why, he can come to live again with my herds.'

'But,' shouted his wife, 'we get no milk from the cows. They have no milk because the big bull keeps all the cows for himself.'

'Every cow shall give you milk from now on,' promised the Mayor, to everybody's astonishment. It was one thing to lead the big bull away, but quite another to promise,

35

before everybody, that Mr Weich's herd of cows would, in future, give milk when everybody knew that they had for so long refused. They stared at their Mayor. He, however, seemed quite serious for, after all, had the cows not promised him that they would all give milk and had promised, on their honour, there in the moonlight with the tears still wet on their long eyelashes?

That is really the end of the story. Except, of course, to tell you that the Mayor walked slowly to Mr Kämpfer, talking all the time in a very low voice.

'Mr Kämpfer,' he said. 'I have just come to you from the home where you were born.' And Mr Kämpfer listened while the Mayor explained how every cow and every bull – even Mr Feigling – wanted to welcome him back as their leader. 'King Bull,' the Mayor called him, 'you were born to lead. Well, I mean – you cannot fight people who are determined to accept you as their friend and leader, can you?'

Mr Kämpfer had never heard a human speak like this. Not only could he understand the man but the voice held no fear, only a wonderful friendship, and told of a welcome waiting in the green fields the bull so much loved.

And that is how, watched by everybody, Mr Kämpfer allowed himself to be led away quietly, out of the ring and along the lane and back to the herd awaiting their leader.

As you will know the cows kept their promise and the milkmaids came running, one after the other, to tell their mistress, Mrs Weich, that there were not enough milk pails to collect all the milk. And such milk you never did taste. It was the whitest, creamiest, most nourishing liquid ever poured down a human throat.

36

'And another thing,' said a milkmaid to her ploughman that very evening. 'Every bull has its own cow. Isn't that strange?' To which her ploughman replied 'Well I never did! It fairs beats cock-fighting, don't it?'

And, if you happen to go that way when you are older, and want a drink of the whitest, sweetest, creamiest and most nourishing drink you will ever have why, just pop into the Kingdom of Waxindioren, go south until you reach the little town of Poppycock and ask around for the farm of Mr Kämpfer. You cannot mistake the place. Just look around and you will see a field where each contented cow will be with her contented husband and all the young cows look up every now and then and gaze admiringly and longingly at the magnificent physique of their leader. And, as you cross that field – and you need not be afraid to do so – you will see at the far end of the cows' sheds a special barn, separate from the others. Over the door is a board, of which Mr Kämpfer is very proud, and which reads: **'MR KÄMPFER, MONARCH OF ALL BULLS. THE BEST MILKER OF THEM ALL.'**

The King's Lion

Oh, lovely people of my heart! As you drop off to sleep this night let your thoughts travel to Poppycock, with the clock put back to an evening in June. The air is full of the scents of the trees, the flowers and the different kinds of grasses. One can hear the sound of the bees still busy visiting the flowers, which have not yet closed for the night.

Mayor Dowmen von Popo-lock is standing on the balcony of his fine house which overlooks the ocean – well it is the sea really, for the straits just across the road are but a mile from the open sea. The sound of the water is a background to life in this house; and only the clip-clop of horses' hooves and the rumble of carriage wheels passing by break the peace and quiet of the place.

The Mayor is contented in a very special way. Recent occasions have brought prosperity to the little town of Poppycock. People from all over the Kingdom of Waxindioren come to visit the town where so many wonderful happenings occur.

'There they are,' they say, pointing to the two knights on the entrance to the town. And it is not long before they are buying tickets to stay up and try to see the knights change places. And then there is the boat place,

39

the metal plaque on the ground showing the very spot on which Poppycock tried to feed its baby boat. Of course, no one would come to Poppycock without that greatest of all experiences – a visit to see Mr Kämpfer, the bull. Such an interesting place and no wonder its Mayor, the lordly Dowmen von Popo-lock, is very proud.

Suddenly a pigeon flew onto the balcony and stood panting and staring at the Mayor who, recognising the gold seal around its neck, hastened to open the little purse and take out the message.

Now I should tell you that, in those days, before the invention of the telephone, pigeons carried messages, and right well they did it and much cheaper than our modern postage.

'Don't break my neck in your eagerness,' said the pigeon. 'I've got to get back as quickly as I can with your reply. The King himself said so.'

The Mayor was staring at the message. He could hardly believe what it said.

'Why does he send for me?' he said softly, wonderingly and apprehensively to himself. 'I am not a doctor. I've no knowledge of medicine.'

'It's your own fault,' said the pigeon hastily. 'Just think how you pretended to cure the Queen's cat.'

'Pretended!' said the Mayor angrily. 'I didn't pretend. I made it quite well.'

'More fool you,' said the pigeon rudely, because she hated cats, who chase all birds. 'So now you must go and cure the King's lion.' And the pigeon giggled and chuckled with great enjoyment.

'You've been reading top secret messages... I could have you shot for that,' said the Mayor crossly.

40

'You'd be much better advised to give yourself to solving your own problem,' replied the pigeon wisely. 'Anyway, I must be off, back to the palace. Best get your reply written,' and the pigeon hopped about on one leg, shaking with laughter.

'Be quiet, you foolish, fat flea-pit of feathers!' said the Mayor, going indoors to a desk and picking up a quill.

The pigeon followed the Mayor, who scratched his head as always when deep in thought, then quickly wrote his reply.

'Most Noble Majesty,' he wrote. 'Of course, I shall hasten to cure your lion. I am leaving at once and will come with all possible speed.' Then, again scratching his head, he turned to the pigeon.

'You must have seen many such letters to his Majesty?' The pigeon nodded his head to agree that it was so. 'Then how does one end?'

The Mayor obviously hated having to ask but the pigeon was delighted to hear the question.

' "Your humble servant",' explained the pigeon, sticking out its chest as only pigeons can.

And so it was that one hour later, after much hurry and bustle among the household of the Mayor, the lordly Dowmen von Popo-lock, accompanied by Doctor Unterschnell, who had left the undertaker, Mr Freethorf, in charge, left the little town of Poppycock on the journey to the palace of the King and Queen of Waxindioren.

Now I must tell you people who love me like I love you that Mayor Dowmen von Popo-lock had brought this journey upon himself by pretending to cure the Queen's Cat.

You will know that the King had summoned him to

41

the palace to explain why the taxes had not been paid. You will remember that he had made a return visit, taking not only one year's tax but two, and a beautiful present for the Queen. It was on this latter visit that he had made friendly conversation with the Queen's cat, who presented a great chance to deepen the lady's appreciation of her loyal citizen Mayor.

'I saw how they treat one when one is ill,' said the cat, who had taken an instant liking to the Mayor because of the way he wore his periwig, 'so I decided on a few days of it myself. Breakfast in bed, extra milk, absolute quiet. It's marvellous, but I've decided to get better tomorrow. Too long becomes boring.'

'Do you mind if I pretend to cure you?' asked the Mayor. The cat looked at the Mayor and admired him for his shrewdness.

'Not in the least,' said the Cat. 'In fact I'll pretend this very afternoon to be much worse. Then you can come and make me better. Pretend to mix a magic potion and I'll drink it and, after a nap, be quite cured.'

'I'll mix you the nicest drink you ever had,' said the Mayor, gratefully warming to the deception, because he enjoyed play-acting and could see great benefit for himself in the plan.

So the Queen's favourite cat became much worse; and the Queen quite distraught; and the doctors by the half-dozen were summoned but none could help. And by chance the good Mayor Dowmen von Popo-lock happened on the scene and took in the situation at a glance.

'Have you attended to the cat's pabulatums?' he asked the poor bewildered doctors in front of all the Court. Now you will know, as did the Mayor, that none of the doctors had the least idea what a pabulatum could be but, being men of learning, not one of them would admit the fact. The Mayor dismissed them from the palace, whereupon thirty doctors rushed home to their books to find out what a pabulatum could possibly be.

Meanwhile, the learned Mayor of Poppycock sent for a dish into which he mixed three whole eggs and one small jar of honey, all beaten together with the creamiest of milk. This he did with great show but without anyone having the least idea of what had gone into the medicine, for he had also ordered many other strange things which were later apparently partially used. He then poured the medicine into a bottle which he presented to the Queen.

'Give your cat three saucers of the cure,' he said. 'By the end of the third saucer your beloved cat will be well. Quite recovered,' and, with the air of a genius, the Mayor retired to await results.

Of course, the cat drank the milk and honey and, after a very pleasant nap, wakened, yawned, stretched and sprang into the lap of his Queen, who was beside herself with joy which quickly turned to gratitude. Grabbing a sword from a Gentleman-in-Waiting she rushed into the room where the Mayor rested and would have knighted him on the spot except that he, on whom all honour was to be bestowed, saw the sword in the hand of the excited woman and fled through the window hoping to save his life. When, at last, he was found, the King declared that he alone could make a knight and so the Mayor of Poppycock remained unknighted.

And now he had to set out to cure the King's lion! 'May heaven preserve me,' he thought for the thousandth time. 'I tremble at the thought, for a cat is one thing but a lion quite another.'

'It is only a cat, but bigger,' said Doctor Unterschnell, trying to enjoy the journey and cheer up his Mayor and mentor. But the Mayor only glared at him and said that he was the biggest fool in the whole kingdom.

Twenty leagues before the palace the Mayor halted the caravan of wagons and bade camp to be made for the night, with the excuse that they could all arrive fresh in the morning.

'Simply wants to delay meeting his patient,' laughed Doctor Unterschnell behind the Mayor's back. But you and I know that there was a better reason. What am I saying? Who can have a better reason than to delay meeting a lion?

Anyway, we know that the Mayor set off alone to meet the foxes in the field of his pabulatums but, to his dismay, they were not there. He was not to know it but the day was Vulpesenden, which is a Bank Holiday for all foxes.

So, without help, advice or any kind of comfort the Mayor, at the head of his party, entered the palace gates with certain knowledge that he would not live through that day without having to meet the lion.

'See how upright he is,' said the Queen to her husband as they watched the party from Poppycock enter the gates.

'Let's see how upright he is when he meets my Leo face to face,' said the King, secretly hoping that the Mayor would flee for his life.

The Mayor, on being shown to his room, was delighted to be met by the Queen's cat.

44

'The whole Court is waiting to have sport at your expense,' said the cat, as soon as they were alone together. 'Only the Queen has faith in your abilities ... and myself, of course.' The cat laughed. The Mayor did not see what there was to laugh about for, as he walked to the window and gazed out across the beautiful sloping lawns at the rear of the palace, he could see the large iron cage which was the home of Mr Leo, the King's pet lion. And there he was – a great lumbering mass of yellow African lion.

'Don't look so down-hearted,' said the cat. 'I helped you once. I'll help you again.' So saying he bade the Mayor sit down and listen most carefully.

'Leo is a cat, like I am,' explained the cat. 'He is bigger and is the King of all the animals, but he is still a cat. That is how I understand him perfectly. Now you must understand that there are two kinds of us animals. Some of us have learned to live with man and to tolerate him – even to like him at times. The others have never learned to accept humans as harmless and would rather kill them than trust them. Do you understand?'

The good Mayor nodded his head to show that it was so.

'Fear – that's what it's all about,' continued the cat. 'Now, you can talk with me; why not with Leo?'

'Go and talk to a lion?' exclaimed the Mayor. 'Come now, Mr Whiskers. Would you have me killed? We have been such good friends.'

Mr Whiskers put out his paw and the Mayor saw that the claws were out. As quick as a flash the cat stroked them right down the Mayor's face but, though the razor sharp claws actually touched the skin, they only tickled,

45

and the movement was a harmless caress, not an attack.

'There,' said the cat. 'I am small, so you have no fear of me, yet I have teeth and claws just like Mr Leo. I could have done you a serious injury, but why should I? As you say, you are my friend. Now, why should Mr Leo wish to hurt you any more than I? And, to make quite certain, I have been and told Mr Leo about you.'

'You have made an arrangement like we had?' asked the Mayor, for the first time beginning to feel his days were not to be counted in ones.

'I have made an arrangement with Leo,' said the cat.

'What do I have to do?' asked the Mayor.

'You must do a bit of play-acting first,' said the cat. 'You have to convince everyone, and especially the King, how brave and clever you are...'

'But I'm not brave and...'

'Clever,' said the cat. 'Yes, I know you are a coward and rather stupid, but only the animals know that – so, listen carefully to what I tell you. The lion is in love. He wants to visit a lady lion he met once before when he had his claws trimmed and his teeth cleaned.'

'I can't get him that,' said the Mayor.

'Just be quiet and learn what we have arranged,' said the cat. And so the lordly Mayor Dowmen von Popolock heard and learned what to do. He only hoped that what the cat said was true for, if not, the good town of Poppycock would most assuredly be needing a new Mayor.

'I do hope I can remember all you say,' said the Mayor, knowing how he always needed to be prompted in everything he did.

The cat sighed. These humans were so feeble-minded. 'Leo will prompt you if you can't remember,' he assured

46

the anxious Mayor. 'Now go and get on with convincing the King and the Court. The Queen already has faith in your non-existent abilities.'

So, with all the Courtiers and their King and Queen watching from the safety of the rooms overlooking the lawns where Leo lived in his cage, the brave Mayor Popo waved and bowed and then approached the cage.

The moment had arrived. Leo raised his massive head and yawned. His mouth was so big and his teeth so large and so many! Then, as arranged, Leo stood erect and roared. The sound was louder than thunder and never had the Mayor been so petrified with fear. The look and sound of the beast made everyone's heart miss a beat. The ladies' bosoms shook off their binding buttons and the men gasped and made wind in their breeches. It was awful, yet the brave Mayor lifted the latch and entered the lion's cage.

'Hello,' said the lion. 'I've been waiting for you since yesterday.'

'I was held up,' said the Mayor. 'What do we do now?'

'I'm going to open my mouth and you must put your head right inside and have a good look around. Then you must go and tell the King that my teeth need scraping.'

The Mayor remembered what the cat had said. 'Put your head right in. Make sure that everybody sees you do it. That's important. Everybody must see how brave you are. They'll do anything you say after that.'

'My friend Sheeba is having her nails clipped and her teeth cleaned at the vet's,' explained the lion. 'You must persuade the King to send me there tomorrow.'

So the lion opened its mouth and the brave Mayor

put his head right inside. The lion partly closed his mouth and, for a moment, their Majesties and all the Courtiers thought that was to be the end of the Mayor. But Leo had done it only to make the action look more real and dangerous. He was as careful as the cat had been not to hurt the Mayor.

'I must say you need something cleaned,' said the Mayor. 'Your breath is putrid.' The lion was not offended. He thought the Mayor's words funny so he roared out loud with laughter. The whole world seemed to shake. Never had the onlookers heard such a fearsome noise. The King and Queen were astonished to see the brave Mayor Popo simply pat Leo on his massive head and, with a final waggle of a finger at the lion, come back to make his report.

'His teeth are giving trouble, Sire,' said the Mayor. 'He must have them cleaned without delay.'

The Queen quite forgot her dignity in brimful admiration of her subject, the Mayor. She kissed him on each cheek and that was as good as being knighted on the spot.

And that is how the fame of the little town of Poppycock grew and grew. Who else had a Mayor so clever and so brave, for not only did Popo do the deeds of which I have told you but many more – such as meeting Leo's friend, the lioness Sheeba, who entered fully and instantly into the game with a few additions of her own – but that is another story and you will not want to hear it now, for you must think over this story carefully or you will miss some of the finer points of the Mayor's bravery.

Treats

The lordly Mayor Dowmen von Popo-lock was giving the matter his undivided attention. Well – not exactly. He was, in fact, fast asleep.

It just would not be proper to give an instant agreement, even though such authority was vested in the august, fat, lazy but benign gentleman who now lay asleep in the Mayor's Parlour.

Mr Teerleber, the owner of the circus, was not annoyed, for he knew the ways of these officials and so had settled himself resignedly to wait. He knew that, if he was patient, he would be rewarded. And so it was. The Mayor awakened, performed his pabulatums, drank a glass of rine water (which he was certain kept his bowels in good order), and then told the Beadle that he was ready to see the circus owner.

The weighty matter took only a few moments. The circus would send a carriage for the Mayor and a few Councillors, who would visit the circus at its present venue. If all was well, permission would be granted for a whole week in Poppycock.

The Mayor chose his companions carefully. Some of them he ruled out without much thought. He could not possibly be accompanied by old DickKopf, for the man's mind had, somehow, been omitted at birth! Councillor

Bloomen was a good companion but would never leave his flower shop for a whole day for such a frivolous and pleasure-seeking occasion. Councillor Kniper, who owned the local public house, would be most pleasant company but, because he was not allowed a drink while on duty in his own establishment, would certainly drink himself silly and be a burden to the party. Councillor Gicht suffered bouts of gout, and a bout of gout might spoil the occasion. 'There's nowt like a bout o' gout fer stoppin' a man goin' out,' old Gicht said often, when the irritation made him lapse back into the dialect of his childhood.

So the lordly Mayor Dowmen von Popo-lock, wearing his chain of office and accompanied by four of his Councillors – Dr Unterschnell, Mr Freethorf, Mr Kahl and Mr Schmerz – were welcomed by the circus owner, Mr Teerleber, and were introduced to the artists whose skills nightly thrilled and entertained the public. There was no time actually to see the performance: not if the real business of the visit was to be properly fulfilled. As soon as the introductions were over the guests were conducted to the buffet-bar where a sumptuous meal was served, with the best cigars and wine unlimited. The management of Teerleber's knew how to make certain of their next planned venue.

After a few hours of drinking and gourmandising it would have seemed churlish to refuse to join in the favourite games of the circus folk. Innocent folk, they played simple games. Dr Unterschnell seldom prayed but did so silently but fervently as he had a cigarette lashed out of his mouth by the Ringmaster's whip. Worse was to follow. Mr Freethorf was thinking of the very best oak – no ordinary pine box for him – as he politely stood, terrified, while an apple was shot from his head by the leader of the shooting team. The Mayor suggested a game of Twirl the Trenchard but, seeing that the idea did not appeal, slipped quietly away and sought out the circus animals, with whom he would feel much more comfortable and who did not play such dangerous and stupid games.

The place was easily located because of the smell. A long row of cages and, at each end, the tethered animals whose habits were more tolerant of man.

'Vot you vant 'ere?' asked the little man called Mahout, who looked after the elephants. 'I sees you is a Mayor but yous not allowed 'ere. Pleez; you goes back upstairs wheres you belongs?'

'What is that stuff you are giving the elephants?' asked the Mayor. 'It looks exactly like the stuff that grows in such profusion at the back of my house.'

The Mahout stared at the Mayor. 'Stuff?' he said. 'That's treats. Poppy seed, 'ash. It grows anywheres. I mix it with wot I can get. You ask upstairs. Pleez; you go now.'

The Mayor had no alternative. He was ushered upstairs and back to the party.

'What is that stuff your man gives to the elephants?' he asked the manager as they all prepared to leave.

'Cattle cake, hay, seed,' answered the man.

'But... The poppy seed, hashish...'

'Oh,' laughed the manager quietly. 'Between you and me, we have to give the animals treats now and then. You know – hash, cannabis, charas, ganja, bbang, you name it, whatever we can get hold of. Quietens 'em down, y'know. Couldn't do without something of the kind, especially when the old bull gets musth.'

52

The Mayor was very thoughtful on the journey back to Poppycock. A field of poppy seed was growing in great profusion just behind his house! Treats! Remarkable, quite remarkable.

An advance party arrived to prepare the circus ground. The inhabitants of Poppycock watched all this with profound interest and anticipation. Only the grandmas and grandpas had seen a circus and now, within a few days, they would be paying their Pengels and sitting on those rows of wooden seats they now saw being erected.

They thought affectionately of their good Mayor Dowmen von Popo-lock. How clever he was to arrange the entertainment. How sensible to charge a fee so that their little town would not be caused expense. How conscientious to the benefits of Poppycock going all that way to Trara merely to inspect the circus and make sure that it was of a quality suitable for the good people of Poppycock. No town could ever have known a better Mayor; a man of honour, whose bravery had been proven – for everyone knew how he had confronted the King's lion; whose skill was undoubted – for they had all learned of how their Mayor had cured the Queen's cat; how compassionate – for had he not returned the little boat to its mother? and how astute with the town's finances – for the two knights still changed places and brought in tourists from all over the Kingdom of Waxindioren. And now this circus which, so it was said, had brought the finest zoo that any circus had ever put together. Yes, Poppycock appreciated the lordly Mayor Dowmen von Popo-lock. Some, and especially the ladies, felt even stronger and loved the man. Two things were certain.

He had no enemies and people never tired of hearing of his doings and exploits.

And so it came to pass. The circus opened and there they all sat; special seats for special people.

Doctor Unterschnell was with his tall, thin wife who always insisted on being called Mrs Doctor, though she did not know a tibia from a fibula and thought them both in the head.

Then there was Mr Freethorf, whose wife looked as though she had been sat upon at birth. Do not ask why, but that is how she looked. Never had she been known to smile and it was difficult to know whose face was the longer, Mrs Freethorf's or her husband's.

They say that, if people live long enough together, they grow to look like each other. Well, Mr and Mrs Kniper, who owned the public house opposite the Town Hall, looked so alike that, if they had changed his breeches for her skirts, no one would have noticed.

Not so Mr and Mrs Kahl. His head was without hair. He was completely bald but his wife had hair that stood up in spikes and could well have been used as a door mat.

Mrs Schmerz, the dentist's wife, was elegant. She had known the benefit of a good education and could both read and write, and even spell words correctly. At the KLUGER School she had shown early abilities and been made a monitor, as befits the future wife of a professional man.

However, Mrs Bloomen, like her husband, had no superior airs and graces, but they both had green fingers and everything they planted grew perfectly as intended. Their florist's shop was a delight to see and to smell and graced the little town of Poppycock.

Next to Mr Bloomen sat Mr and Mrs DickKopf. They did not look alike but they were equally dim-witted. Sometimes, when the Mayor told a joke in the bar after a Council meeting, Mr DickKopf would scratch his head and ponder. Then, the next day, when he was having his dinner in the evening, he would laugh out loud because the point of the joke had quite suddenly pierced through to his well-insulated understanding. He would retell the joke to his wife, who would smile, but without comprehension. But, sure enough, that night she would wake her husband with her laughter, for the point of the joke would have found its way through the armour plating of her faculties.

So they sat under the huge marquee, watching the good and the bad, as trapeze artists performed daring feats and the animals were made to do their acts, while stunted dwarfs did their best to amuse by clowning for their daily bread.

The Lady Mayoress had been mightily put out to see the great bull elephant get excited, for its anatomy is an awesome sight for a lady whose husband is such an inattentive dreamer as the lordly Mayor who sat by her side.

It strolled around the ringside as part of the act, taking sweets, fruit and nuts from the audience. One woman had thought to be clever and had given the elephant a tub of ice cream. He blew it straight back at her and everybody but she thought the act a marvellous joke.

Then the Ringmaster, who looked so splendid in his red coat and black breeches but had the nervous habit of constant manducation, which made people think he was perpetually eating his dinner, announced a special treat and into the ring came a lady elephant followed by her baby, who held tightly to his mother's tail. It was a pretty sight. Everyone gasped out their joy at the sight and searched their programmes to find the name of the youngest elephant they had ever seen.

Now Pachyderm had been given the name by his mother because she thought to have such a grand name would give her son a good start in life. But nobody had been able to say such a long name. I mean, fancy having to call him in for a meal and having to shout 'Pachyderm, Pachyderm. Your dinner is ready.' So they shortened the name to Pachy, and that became Packy, and everybody believed he was an Indian elephant, though his mother truly came from Burma.

Many people believe that elephants have good memories and never forget. That is sometimes so, but not always. Little Packy was different. He never could remember. He forgot everything as soon as he was told. It was his mother's fault for she was just as forgetful. The little fellow was constantly being lost, and that is why he had to hold on to his mother's tail. If he absent-mindedly forgot and let go and she wandered off for some reason or other then Packy was lost and that was why the monkeys were constantly bringing him back to his mum, who mostly had even forgotten she had a son.

And that is how Packy came to wander off after the show and a herd of cows in a field near Poppycock looked up to find this funny-looking stranger in their midst.

'He has the longest nose I've ever seen,' said Daisy, but the grass was so green and sweet that she instantly forgot about unimportant things like a young elephant eating beside her and her little calf.

56

The man called Mahout, who was paid to look after the elephants, suddenly noticed that Packy was missing.

'Ver ist yor son?' he shouted at Packy's mother, though she was not deaf. 'If you've lost him again I'll never give you another treat of seed,' he threatened, and you who have never owned an elephant already know that the seed of the poppy is useful for calming an elephant, especially when having its feet pedicured.

As the show ended and everyone rose to go Popo was in deep thought and had to be told that it was time to go home.

'Go on ahead,' he told his wife, the Mayoress. 'Take the official carriage. I'll walk home later.'

As soon as the Mayoress had departed Popo went alone under the sloping seats in search of the animals' quarters.

Perhaps you do not remember, or maybe you were not there when I told you, but Mayor Dowmen von Popo-lock knew how to talk to animals. His mother, who had been the prettiest girl in the whole of Poppycockland, had taught him as a child. She was the seventh child of a lady who had also been a seventh child and not only that, but both had six fingers on their left hands, which is a sure sign of having special gifts and of being more than ordinary mortals.

The lions roared their boredom at the lone man who passed their cage, and the Bengal tiger spat the defiance of his hatred of all things human.

'Be still and make less noise,' said Popo-lock quietly. The lions were bewildered and the tiger immediately stopped its pacing. Never had a human voice spoken their language so that they could understand every word.

'Who said that?' shouted a huge gorilla in the cage at the end of the row.

'I did,' said Popo-lock. 'And I suggest that you stop your shouting. If you bring other humans around I shall not be able to talk with you all.'

'It's jiggery-pokery,' screamed one of the monkeys. 'It's not right or normal that a human should be able to talk our language' and the monkey came as close as he could and, peering intently, said softly to Popo-lock 'You are a human, I suppose?'

'Be silent, you ugly creature,' said the tiger, who was totally intrigued.

'I am sorry to see you all in such confined places,' said Popo-lock. 'But I dare not free you for you would all be shot as dangerous.'

'Shot as dangerous!' the monkeys screamed together in chorus.

'Yes. I know about that,' said the tiger. 'They use long sticks. The men point them and they make a loud noise; then one's mother dies. It's how I came to be here.'

All the animals stared at the tiger. Never before had he spoken, only roared and cursed everybody and everything. Now he looked quiet and pathetic. All the animals felt sympathy. They could imagine the little tiger cub licking and trying to rouse his shot-dead mother.

Suddenly a voice far above them all aired an opinion.

'They wouldn't shoot me. I'm too valuable,' said the giraffe.

'Oh, be quiet, you elongated, bog-eyed weirdo,' said one of the little donkeys, who had always envied the lofty size and dignity of the giraffe.

'Let us be polite to each other,' said Popo-lock. 'I am not the most important among you but I'm the one who is free so, if you want me to talk to you, be polite and, above all, be quiet or someone will hear and I shall have to go.'

'Don't go,' said the gorilla. 'Open these cages and set us all free. Then we can go back where we came from – home.' The gorilla had worked himself into a frenzy and, taking hold of the bars of his cage, he shook them until the whole cage rattled.

'If you won't be quiet I shall leave you,' said Popo-lock firmly, so that even the gorilla opened his mouth to be quiet in amazement.

'Aren't you frightened of me?' he asked, disbelievingly.

'There is a difference between being daft and being demonic,' said Popo-lock. 'You are just being daft,' – and he turned his back on the gorilla's cage and spoke to all the other animals.

'Vot you doin' 'ere?' said the Mahout, who had just come back from searching the circus for Packy. ''Ave you seen a baby elephant?' The man stared at the lordly figure of Popo-lock, who was wearing the Mayoral chain of office round his neck. 'Oh!' he gasped. 'It's you! I'm sorry, your reverence. We've lost Packy, the baby of the show.'

At the approach of Mahout all the animals resumed their former attitudes and behaviour. The tiger spat out his hatred, the lions roared, the monkeys chattered, the giraffe stared heavenwards, the horses continued eating, the leopard crouched, the gorilla growled and the camels looked disinterested and aloof. Only the elephant showed affection, for she reached out her long nose, called a

59

trunk, and felt to find out what the brown-skinned little man might have in his pockets.

'There has been no baby here all the time I've been here,' said the Mayor. 'He's probably wandered off and is somewhere in the area. Have a quick look around and, if you can't find him, I'll come and help.'

'I knew I should have chained him like I do his mother,' said Mahout as he went off to search for Packy.

'Now, listen,' said the Mayor, and all the animals immediately stopped their natural noises and listened attentively to this peculiar human who could convey his thoughts as if he was a full member of their own fraternity.

'I am the Mayor of this town. If you all do your best while you are here I shall see to it that you have more food and I shall come often to talk to you all. If you have any special requests I shall try to fulfil your needs.'

'Open the cages and set us free,' said the gorilla again. 'I'm fed up being in this little cage. It's not like being free.'

'I'm free,' bleated a goat at the end of the row. 'I'm free because I'm sensible and don't go around frightening everybody with loud roars.'

'I'm free because I'm beautiful,' said the giraffe.

'I'm free because they forgot to click the cage shut,' said the leopard, at which statement the Mayor hastily shut the cage door which the leopard had just found was not properly shut.

'Why did you do that?' asked the leopard angrily.

'You are supposed to be locked up,' said the Mayor. 'You noticed your cage door was not locked only because we were talking about freedom.'

'You are no friend of mine,' snorted the leopard.

'If you were free what would you do?' asked the Mayor reprimandingly.

'He'd eat us,' chorused the monkeys.

'And you?' asked the Mayor of the lions.

'They'd eat me,' said the leopard.

'And you, King Tiger? Who would you eat?' asked the Mayor.

'I don't eat other animals, only meat,' said the tiger, who had been in captivity as long as he could remember.

'Let me out and I'll run straight back to where I came from,' said the gorilla. 'Thick bushes and trees there were. Lovely things to eat. Fruit, berries...'

'Shut your big silly mouth,' shrieked the monkeys. 'They brought you on a ship. You would be lost immediately, just as we would.' And, turning to the Mayor apologetically and pointing at the gorilla, the King monkey said, 'He's daft, but he's harmless.'

'Listen, all of you,' said the Mayor. 'If I could buy you all I'd set you in proper grounds like your natural homes. But, if you were all free now, you'd starve or be shot. You animals kill for two reasons only: fear and hunger. Humans, I'm sorry to say, kill for what they call sport. You're better where you are, but I'll see you get more food. Meanwhile, talk to each other. Try to be friends'. And the good and lordly Mayor left the animals talking to each other for the first time instead of screaming or roaring abuse.

As the Mayor strolled home he saw, across the fields, a sight strange enough to stop any lovely person in his tracks. A homely scene – a herd of his friends the cows, each with their own husband and children grazing peacefully but lifting their heads as ordered by Mr Kämpfer in greeting to the Mayor. But, as his gaze took in the scene, his mind refused to believe what his eyes saw. There, amongst the cattle, was the missing baby Packy. It was all so peaceful and not a cow nor a bull nor a calf showed surprise at the elephant standing in their midst. If the cattle could so naturally accept an elephant would it be possible...? Could he bring about...?

Suddenly there was a great noise, a shouting, a hullabaloo. Dowmen von Popo-lock stood quite still. Fear rooted him to the spot. Charging down the hill at unbelievable speed was the bull elephant. The trumpeting he was making must surely be frightening the two stone knights on their perches in the centre of Poppycock. It certainly terrified Popo, who regained mobility and ran for his life.

What was he doing? Was he mad? He blinked and came mentally and physically to life. He was running after the elephant – in the same direction!

Just as Popo realised this terrible error he was seen by thirty villagers who shut their doors and slid the bolts to give a feeling of security. If their Mayor was giving chase all would be well: brave fellow. Soon the circus staff were seen, but all well behind the brave Mayor who, going downhill, had neither the strength nor the ability to stop. Somehow terror made his limbs work. He nearly caught up with the elephant, whose trumpeting blasted the countryside like a foghorn.

As both elephant and Mayor crested the hill and disappeared from view Popo reached the safety of his house, ran in and closed the door with a great thud. The Lady Mayoress had witnessed the marathon and had been astonished at her husband's bravery.

'Oh, you brave man!' she cried, taking the shivering Mayor into her embrace.

'Brave?' he stuttered, trying hard to regain his composure and not a little puzzled at this turn of events. As the blood cooled and his breathing became normal the lordly Mayor Dowmen von Popo-lock slowly realised what his wife had said. Brave? She had seen him run for his life! Of course, fear had given him wings and he had run blindly, with no choice of direction. It had been the wrong direction – or had it?

As they stood locked in a most unusual and loving embrace a great crashing could be heard just outside. There, in the field at the end of their garden, stood the great bull elephant. With his trunk he was placidly pulling up the long grass and stuffing massive amounts into his mouth. Popo was amazed and found himself going to the nearest window.

The bull elephant looked peaceful enough and had stopped all his trumpeting, for you cannot bellow defiance with your mouth full of seed. Popo felt a flood of curiosity course where abject fear had been. He opened the conservatory doors and began cautiously, one step at a time, to approach the elephant.

'Do take care,' whispered the Mayoress, by now bursting with pride at her husband's bravery. She could see in the distance many villagers and all the strangers who belonged to the circus. They had reached the brow of the hill but had not ventured any nearer.

Popo came within twenty paces of the great elephant before the animal looked up and said quietly, 'Why are you walking as if your breeches are too tight?

Popo was quite taken aback. 'My breeches fit perfectly,'

he said. 'More to the point, why have you caused such a commotion, run away and charged about like you were mad?'

'I was mad,' said the elephant. 'Musth, you know. I get it when I feel like it.' He continued all the while ramming the poppy seed into his mouth. 'Have some,' he said, in the most comradely manner.

The Mayor declined but was beginning to see the advantages to be had from the situation.

'Where are your wife and your child?' he demanded.

The elephant did not for a moment stop eating but, through tufts of grass and a huge mouthful of seed, muttered that his son was happy amongst the cattle. His wife was safely tethered back at the circus. Everything was most satisfactory and as it should be. It was then that the lordly Mayor saw the huge but broken chain hanging from the great thick foot.

'You've eaten enough,' he said in the most commanding voice he could muster. 'If you ram any more down your gullet you'll be ill.' He expected the elephant to be angry. Instead the great animal looked at him in the most friendly way.

'Let us go back then,' he said. 'I'll let you ride on me if you like.'

So, with everyone watching, the wonderful hero of Poppycock rode the bull elephant back the way they had run, collecting Packy on the way who, this time, held on to his father's tail.

'There's just one thing,' said the elephant before they reached the crowd of admiring people. 'Tell me the truth. You were afraid, were you not?'

The Mayor scratched the back of the elephant's ear

and took a long time to answer. He knew only the truth would do, for animals do not lie to each other. Only humans do that.

'I was terrified,' he admitted and, as they reached the crowd and people surrounded them to welcome their hero, the elephant laughed. He felt in the very best of moods and had enjoyed a wonderful day. It was not every day that he could break a chain, pretend to be mad, frighten everything around – even the other animals – and fill his belly with treats he had never expected to find.

As for the Mayor – you can imagine how the tale grew and grew as it passed from mouth to mouth. No-one could think of an honour great enough, so they gave him nothing. But the Queen sent a message that only a knighthood was fitting to the bravery of this most wonderful Mayor in the whole of her husband's kingdom. That, however, is another story, and it really filled the front pages of every newspaper in the whole of Waxindioren.

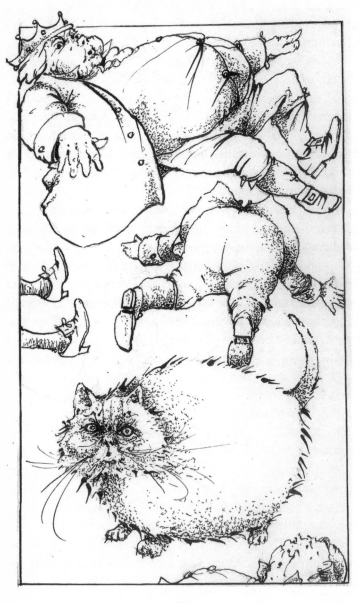

Lake Furzen

It used to be different, but there is no excuse now for not visiting all the countries of the world, and that should always include Waxindioren.

If you were able to look down on that small but magical kingdom you would quickly realise a strange fact, for its shape is like no other.

It looks exactly like a baby bending down, or it could really be anybody bending over; and if you wonder what that focal point is, so far beneath you in the centre of the land and like a musical fermata, it is a lake of the bluest water you ever did see.

And you would want to visit and see for yourself that most wonderful town of Poppycock, where Dowmen von Popo-lock was Mayor, and which still has many mementoes of that remarkable man.

It was in the year of Logyzoo that the longing first manifested itself in action.

'And the lion shall lie down with the lamb,' droned the voice of the Reverend Shwätzer, at which affirmation the very lordly Mayor Dowmen von Popo-lock sat up and shouted aloud his joy.

Of course, not even such a person as Mayor Popo could expect to interrupt a sermon in church without complaint or comment.

67

'What did you say?' asked the Parson. 'Speak up, Sir. You rudely interrupted my sermon for good cause I hope?'

But the Mayor merely smiled, closed his eyes and ruminated while the Parson droned on about some time in the future when impossible happenings between animals were to occur.

As the good people of Poppycock lined up outside the church to salute their Mayor and other dignitaries the Reverend Shwätzer tried to reprimand the Mayor.

'You called out in your sleep, Sir,' he said icily.

'Not so,' answered the Mayor, 'but the lion shall indeed lie down with the lamb. You have my word for it.' And the people who heard wondered mightily, for most had been asleep and had no notion of the meaning.

As the Mayor helped his graceful wife into their carriage he had settled it all in his mind. All he had to do now was to get the Council to agree.

It was not an easy victory. Mr DickKopf was not called thick-head without reason, while Dr Unterschnell became quite obstreperous in his objections.

'You have neither imagination nor belief in me!' shouted the Mayor. 'You object to everything on principle and without constructive criticism.'

'I am a realist,' answered the doctor.

'You are a fool,' said the Mayor.

'I have MD after my name,' shouted the doctor. 'That doesn't mean mentally deficient, either.'

'Are you sure?' asked the Mayor.

However, in the end the Mayor wore them down and it was agreed that an enclosure be built to the Mayor's requirements.

It was the most reckless idea the good Mayor had ever conceived, but once a possibility took hold of his mind there could be no gainsaying him, and so it was this time and would long be remembered.

Please do not think that the good Doctor Unterschnell disliked the Mayor. Only the King disliked the Mayor. It was just that his plan was frightening in the extreme. Never in history had such a thing been attempted. Blood, death, butchery – that is what it would become.

How can you expect a tiger to walk amongst the zebras, or a lion amongst the gazelles? What would you expect to happen to the monkeys if the leopard had his way? Would the fearsome gorilla not mangle whatever chanced his way? The panther had terrified all who had watched and the pumas had spat out hatred of all who came nearby. Even the guard dogs were ferocious and seemed packed full of hate. No – it was madness unlimited and would be terrible to behold.

Yet there was a certain fascination. They had witnessed the Mayor do so many wonders: put his greasy head into the mouth of a lion; tame a great bull elephant out of musth. Anyway, the public would be safe enough. The Council had insisted on the stoutest of barriers around the enclosure. And there was financial gain in charging a sound and profitable entrance fee, for people would come in flocks and from far around, from all over the Kingdom of Waxindioren.

So the good people of Poppycock watched and talked and the coming event reached far and wide and even the Queen felt the need to hear the plan from he on whom it had been so impossible in the past to persuade her husband to confer honour.

Popo had worn his best breeches and the new shoes with real silver on the buckles. The dainty Lady Mayoress had worn her best dress and a new hat specially for the ceremony. It was the most special occasion, for how many times can a Mayor be knighted in one lifetime?

'Only I can make a knight,' the King had insisted. He envied Popo for his popularity. 'And I will not honour that idiot von Popo-lock.'

Such an insult was almost sacrilege in the Queen's ears.

'He is the bravest, kindest, most courteous Mayor in the Kingdom,' answered the Queen angrily. 'You are jealous because of all the clever and brave deeds he has performed. I shall personally put the Garter on him,' she added.

This enraged the King; to think of his wife, the girl he had made Queen, stooping so low as to slide the Garter up the leg of such an imbecile as the Mayor of Poppycock! Well, it would be outrageous and quite beyond the bounds of decorum. No, it should not be.

But, as any man among you will certainly have learned, when a lady is determined a mere male had better agree. The Queen sent out the invitations and no member of the Council was omitted. Even the King had been astonished for, in the exuberance of her first Investiture, the Queen arranged every detail far better than the ancient and hide-bound officials who looked after the King's affairs.

There was antagonism and jealousy galore, for the Queen's advisers were all ladies and the men looked on with wonder and even envy at preparations the like of which their turgid minds had never conceived. First, there were flowers; masses of them everywhere. Then, there was entertainment the like of which had never before been seen at Court. There was to be a sumptuous meal followed by a Ball and music by the most popular of orchestras. And all this to follow the knighting of that awful fellow, the good Dowmen von Popo-lock, Mayor of Poppycock.

The King fumed, the Court advisers observed with mounting anger made worse by their frustration. What was the Court coming to, to allow a female, even if she was the Queen, to plan so extravagantly – and successfully – and abrogate to herself the power of conferring a knighthood? The King had given permission. There was nothing to be done about the situation: or was it really so?

The King's Chief Councillor, who advised on all matters, was beginning to have an idea. He discussed it with all the Court officials and they, at last, felt their frustration slipping away. If it worked all the preparations would be useless. Of course it would work. It would be a simple matter to arrange.

In the middle of the Kingdom was Lake Furzen. Its blue waters were cold and deep, and fish abounded and were easily caught. But none dared to eat the fish. No-one understood why, but whoever ate of the fish put on weight immediately. They almost blew up, as though filled with air. One little fish was enough to make a man double his weight.

I should like to digress for a moment just to tell you a little but important and true story. There was once a man who thought to commit suicide. He could not swim and jumped into the lake and went thud, straight to the

71

bottom. In going down in so deep a lake he could not help but gasp for air and so swallowed some water. The special liquid applied its gaseous properties so rapidly to such terrific volume that the man was shot out of the water and his only injury, apart from shock, was a bump on his head where he hit a tree on landing. If you believe that you would believe anything – but it is a perfectly true account of what happened. It just proves the danger of eating fish from such a lake.

And that is what they sent to Popo or, at least, that is what they thought was sent to the Mayor's table.

The King's housekeeper knew not where the lovely big carp had been caught. She knew only that they were far too nice to send to the Mayor of a little town that was fast growing above itself.

'Put them down there,' she ordered the messenger. 'Here, take these instead.' And the messenger knew only that he had been told to take twelve fish to the Mayor of Poppycock.

You can guess what happened. The King and his courtiers ate the fish. His Queen, who always dieted before a banquet, did not swallow a single mouthful, but bobbed down and gave her plate to her favourite cat. The cat and the courtiers blew up to immense proportions and the King disappeared for a whole week. It is said that he cursed his doctors, every single one, in language of a deeper blue than the waters of the lake. The expertise of his vocabulary cannot be proven, but it is known for certain that the cat hated him when she found out why she had become as big as a dog but felt so ill at the increase. She determined to have revenge, but that is another story.

Meanwhile, the very next day, while the cat, the King and all his sycophants lay and groaned their misery, the lordly figure of Mayor Dowmen von Popo-lock, together with his good lady and a retinue of officials from Poppycock, were to be seen wending their way along the tree-lined drive to the palace, pausing to admire the stout iron railings erected in preparation for the impending event planned by the Mayor and which now brought him to be knighted.

The Queen watched from her window and was full of admiration for the pompous, fat, over-dressed, funny little man whose deeds so held her esteem. She had always felt a strong penchant for bravery in a man, and was quite blind to any failings that might accompany such a virtue. Her eyes saw a tubby, ungainly, rotund figure coming to be knighted, but her mind and emotions served to present a very different picture in her imagination. A hero, a man of massive and well-earned popularity; fearless, full of character and individuality. It would be a pleasure to tap his shoulder with her husband's sword and say, 'Rise, Sir Popo-lock of Poppycock.'

The Queen had been determined to make a knight of the Mayor ever since he had cured her cat. This time, knowing how sensitive to her protection he was – for, on the previous occasion when she had approached him with a sword he had, so he later explained, thought her to be in danger and instantly chased after who or whatever had threatened his Queen – she approached him slowly, decorously, smiling and with the sword held at the harmless-looking trail position.

As she reached the kneeling figure the cat – enormous in his discomfort but determined not to miss the ceremony

– appeared in the main entrance. He looked for all the world like a mountain lion and frightened the good Mayor temporarily out of his wits. Not only Popo-lock but all who saw the cat, massive in his swollen state, believed they had a lion in their midst and, within two shakes of a lion's tail, everyone had run, leaped, jumped or sprung out of sight. The Queen's last sight of her hero was the backside of his breeches – and not even a Queen can knight a backside.

The cat followed the Mayor. As with all cats his quick wits took in the situation within a second. As he reached Popo the Mayor saw, to his immense relief, who the cat really was. 'You've been eating from Lake Furzen,' he said, trying to sound natural.

'You great blubbery coward,' said the cat. 'Come on. For once in your false life tell the truth. You were scared out of your tiny mind. Is it not so? You thought I was a lion, didn't you?'

'Lion!' said Popo, quickly recovering from his total cowardice. 'Of course not. I merely ... I mean to say ... I ...'

'You are hiding here in the thickness of these bushes, have run away and left your good lady, the Mayoress, and your Queen and you still pretend...? Have you no shame?'

'I made you well when you were ill,' said Popo, not knowing what else to say.

The cat smiled. His was beyond doubt the cleverest mind in the kingdom and he was an opportunist of the worst kind.

'Listen to me,' he said. 'You are a selfish, egotistical, cowardly bag of wind, but I like you. You make me laugh. I'll give you a chance to make yourself an even bigger liar than you are now. We'll pretend to fight in front of all the people hiding in the knighting room. Then I'll run away and you go back as the great man of the day – the man who saved his Queen.'

The lordly Mayor Dowmen von Popo-lock was indeed all the things of which the cat accused him, but slow to realise his advantage he was not.

'Mind you,' advised the cat. 'Be careful. I'm full of wind and ate the fish intended for you. I'll tell you about that later. Another thing; my voice has changed. It is quite loud, even frightening.'

'Why are you so good to me?' asked Popo, wondering if he could trust the cat.

'You'll owe me another favour,' said the cat. 'Now, enough talking. Step out in full view and pretend for all you're worth. Make it convincing and the Queen will love you for ever and the King be even more put out. I'll not come back until I'm normal.' So saying he sprang out of the bushes and attacked the Mayor who, still more than a little disturbed and frightened, fell to the ground with the bloated tawny cat on top of him.

The scuffle produced the most awesome noises from the cat who, with another bound, was away and out of sight.

As the terrible 'lion' disappeared into the garden and the dishevelled Mayor staggered indoors, the Ladies-in-Waiting emerged from their hiding places and hugged and praised the fat, cowardly, scratched, soiled figure of the Mayor.

'Out of the way,' ordered the Queen and, before even the Mayoress could reach her husband, the Queen kissed him on either cheek and announced that this was her way of making him a knight.

There was no need for further ceremony. All the guests assembled round the hero, who had fought the 'lion' with nothing but his bare hands. Within minutes the size of the 'lion' had reached gigantic proportions. Some were certain that it had made to attack the Queen and only Popo's bravery had saved her life.

In truth they believed their own stories, for what is more pleasing than to have been present and seen such wonderful deeds?

As night fell and the music of the most popular of orchestras could be heard across the fields and as far as the beautiful blue waters of Lake Furzen, the lordly figure of Sir Dowmen von Popo-lock, Mayor and accredited hero of Poppycock in Waxindioren, could be seen – perspiring, yes, but still on his feet and dancing with no less a person than the Queen.

As they quadrilled the night away the solitary figure of a cat could be seen. Recovered from his distensions and quietly surveying the contortions of his so-called betters, his expression would have spoken volumes to those who can read the feline mind. The fat little man was not only amusing but useful. Mr Whiskers had plans for him. There was the King to deal with, and who better to do it than the buffoon in breeches who now sweated and perambulated grotesquely round the room?

But I must apologise. I started out to tell you of the marvellously unnatural, unbelievable plan which the Mayor had persuaded his Council to accept. I shall have to tell you all about it in the next story.

Freedom

Mr Teerleber was overjoyed. He had spent half his life visiting officials who, because they held the power to grant the privileges sought by the circus owner, had kept him waiting. He had become used to the procedure. This time the circumstances were reversed. Should he keep the good Dowmen von Popo-lock waiting? Or should he...? He could not make up his mind and so he went straight in to meet the Mayor.

'What a pleasant surprise,' he told the Mayor, though it was no surprise at all and he not only had known about the Mayor's visit but was fully informed of its reason. Better to let the man have his say; pull doubtful faces; pretend to consider the pros and cons before agreeing. If the silly fellow wanted to commit suicide well, let him do so. It was all good advertisement and would bring in lots of money. Mr Teerleber was worried about his animals. He really did love them but ... business was business and what was it the good book said? 'It's never a sin if it's profitable.'

'I've come with a very unusual request,' said the Mayor. And so the circus owner and the lordly Mayor of Poppycock talked ... or rather the Mayor did. Mr Teerleber simply listened and rubbed together hands that tingled as he thought of the thousands of Pengels he would take as

people paid for entrance at the Box Office, where he would personally preside.

Mr Teerleber knew that the Mayor had already obtained the agreement of the Council and was, at that very moment, causing thick and strong iron bars to be put around to make an enclosure through which no animal could break. Mr Teerleber had his informers, who told him all about the Mayor's plan. He even knew that the Queen had sent for the little man and knighted him with kisses. It was preposterous but true.

It was rumoured that the King had been away hunting at the time, but Mr Teerleber knew better. He had once fed fish from Lake Furzen to two guard dogs and actually seen them grow to such a size that they had been quite unable to get out of their kennels. But that is another story.

He had learned how the King had demoted the Mayor. As soon as he had recovered from his gluttony with the fish the King had made a declaration throughout the land of Waxindioren: **'Only the King could make a man a Knight. Any other form of conferring the honour was null and void.'**

The Queen had been so angry at the King for breaking his promise that she had moved her apartment to the far end of the palace, away from His Majesty.

Nevertheless, it was politic to please the little man, so Mr Teerleber called him 'Sir' and handed round his best cigars.

After much huffing and puffing an agreement was reached.

'Sir,' said the circus owner as the fat little man lolled again in his carriage, about to return to Poppycock. 'You will not live to regret our arrangement. I'm sure of it. In fact . . .' but, by that time Popo's coachman had whipped up the horses and the carriage was disappearing. '. . . you probably will not have long to live at all.'

The Mayor was not the fool Mr Teerleber thought. He had done his homework thoroughly.

All the animals had been brought, in their cages, to the enclosure which, until the appointed time to come, was sealed from view of the public. And, as we know, the animals had already more than a passing acquaintance with Mayor Popo from the time when the circus had visited Poppycock. This was a furtherance of that time.

You will remember his long conversation with the animals belonging to the circus and the promises he had made. Well, they had all discussed it at the time, but most could remember only that he had promised them something to which they had looked forward with pleasure. And now, here he was again, sauntering towards them all like a true friend.

'Good morning,' he said. 'I told you I should be back. Now listen carefully to what I have planned. We are all in an enclosure. No one can get out.'

'Not even you?' asked a monkey.

'Well. I can,' said the Mayor, 'but that's different. I arranged it all.'

'Special privileges are special privileges,' said the same monkey scornfully.

'Be quiet, you scraggy bundle of fleas,' said a donkey, who loathed all the monkeys because they rode on his back in the circus ring.

'Yes, be silent. Let's hear what he has planned for our benefit,' said the giraffe from her great height.

'Our benefit!' growled the gorilla. 'His benefit, more likely.'

'I have arranged what has never before been tried,' said Popo. 'You shall – all of you who take the oath – be allowed free, within this enclosure. Out of your cages and...'

'I am free,' said the giraffe.

'So am I,' chorused the horses and donkeys.

'None of you is free,' said the Mayor, pointing to the tether each had around it somewhere.

'Well, I mean, I'm not in a cage like...' and the trick-horse pointed a dainty hoof at the tiger, 'he is.'

'Are you suggesting,' said the zebra, 'that I stay in the same place with the lions and tiger? All free together?'

'And we play games with Mr and Mrs Leopard?' said the donkeys.

' 'Twould never work,' said the king monkey. 'There'd be killings galore.'

'Why?' said the Mayor. 'Who's going to do the killing, and why? You lovely creatures kill only for food. You are not like humans who kill for pleasure. If all of you are well fed why should you kill? Think how wonderful it would be to meet and talk with each other. Do what has never before been done. I know your nature could not stand it for long but ... one day! Where's your self-control?'

There was a ruminative silence – well, nearly. The goats bleated, the lions snorted, the tiger examined his claws and the giraffe knelt down the better to assimilate the unusual atmosphere. They had never even contemplated such a happening.

81

The tiger looked at the goats. The nanny looked as though she may be a little tough, while her husband, Billy, looked decidedly uneatable, his long whiskers drooping down and giving him a dissatisfied and inedible appearance. Stripes, the Bengal tiger, had grown up in the Circus. He had never had to stalk for his food. The meat he ate was pushed through the bars of the nearly empty cage and he ate it while they cleaned out his regular living quarters. Yet he could see quite clearly how tender and succulent the two young kids would be. One bite through each of their necks and... Suddenly he felt ashamed.

The lions muttered amongst themselves. They felt bewildered. Roam free! Such a suggestion was preposterous. A pride of lions nuzzling amongst monkeys, goats, rabbits, cattle, that great stupid giraffe and the insolent leopard. Where would their pride be? All other animals were supposed to be afraid of them. No, it would never do. Yet the idea appealed, though they would have to leave their pride behind for the day.

The monkeys chattered amongst themselves until one could not hear oneself speak in their cage. The king monkey turned a very red rear to the outside and called for silence. As befits the likeness to their human cousins it had long ago been decided to rule democratically.

'Those of you who agree to promise on the right, all others on the left,' he ordered. There was no left. Every single monkey rushed to the right, leaving no doubt at all about the outcome. 'That's settled then,' said their leader.

The leopard had been paying great attention to the

monkeys' cage. He knew how well disciplined they were under all their repeated show of disorder. He also knew how clever they were and had often wished he could be as changeable and adaptable. If they thought it a safe and workable idea he would agree and give his word to behave. Anything would be an improvement on the caged life in this circus zoo.

There was no difficulty amongst the elephants. The bull knew the Mayor quite well. Had he not fed almost to bursting point in the man's garden? It would be pleasant to wander about and show off his harem against the insignificant little creatures like monkeys, donkeys, goats, zebras and the like.

'Are we ready to take the oath?' asked the Mayor. It seemed a simple matter but took a long time. Each animal swore on the sacred sign of Agathodim – and no animal would dare break such a serious vow – to be entirely peaceful, no matter what the provocation.

Not to argue, fight, hurt, molest, insult or in any way interfere with any other animal while free in the enclosure. It was a solemn ceremony and not a single animal remained unimpressed.

'I am very proud of you all,' said the Mayor. 'It will be the greatest occasion in the whole of animal history. You will all be remembered forever.'

So all the animals were given as much food as they could eat and the crowds came from far and near to witness what no-one could believe could be successful.

The incredible events of that day were chronicled in detail in the *Poppycock Gazette*. Within its faded pages lies the following, written by the most famous reporter of the time, Mr Leserschreibe:

Unbelievable, astounding, historic. The people of this land have today witnessed sights their grandchildren will find difficulty in believing.

In a specially built enclosure, and entirely free, was the entire animal population of Teerleber's Circus. The lions walked around quietly and majestically amongst goats, donkeys, monkeys, zebras, horses and every other kind of natural enemy. A haughty giraffe strolled fearlessly with a Bengal tiger, who allowed a gorilla to search his ears for fleas.

In all, I counted sixty-two animals of various species mingled together without anger or assault of any kind. And . . . wait for it, the most unbelievable sight of all. The Mayor of Poppycock not only entered the enclosure but stroked, petted, spoke to and otherwise made friends with all the animals.

Seeing me, and knowing I am a special correspondent, he called out, inviting me to join him in the enclosure. In front of the huge crowd who had paid for entrance how could I refuse?

I thought I should die of fright but entered the enclosure on the promise of the Mayor that I should come to no harm.

I actually touched both a gorilla and the tiger. The lions moved away but, according to Mayor Dowmen von Popo-lock, this was not meant to be offensive but merely because the beasts could not tolerate my smell! So long as I live I shall never be able to forget the experience.

And then a lady from the spectators took up the challenge. The young woman entered the enclosure walking hand in hand with Mayor Popo-lock. I have tried to find this female. On leaving the enclosure she disappeared into the crowd. It was only one experience among so many on that memorable day.

Other famous reporters were present and wrote about

84

the event, but I quote from Mr Leserschreibe because he was the most famous of them all.

The moment had arrived. The crowd watched with bated breath as the fat, ridiculous-looking Mayor of Poppycock entered the enclosure and walked to each cage in turn. The horses, zebras, giraffe, guard dogs, sheep, a cow kept for milk with its calf, several goats and even a little miniature pony, already free, watched as intently as did all the humans as the Mayor released the monkeys. Out they came, scampering into the centre of the enclosure. Then the Mayor opened the gorilla's cage. With one bound he was out and free; standing and staring, obviously not knowing what to do with his freedom. Suddenly he beat his breast and cried out in a loud voice 'I am the greatest. The greatest, do you hear? The greatest!'

The Mayor paused before opening the next cage. He could hear the fear in the gorilla's voice.

'The greatest pudding-head here,' he said to the gorilla. 'Stop bawling and help me undo the cages.' At once the gorilla became quiet. He followed the little fat man and actually opened the next cage, which was that of the leopard.

'Come on, you spotted critter,' said the gorilla politely. 'Come and help undo the cages.'

As each animal was released so it joined the procession, not knowing what else to do with the newly-won freedom. There is a lesson to be learned from this, but that is another story.

There was a very audible gasp of excitement as the lions were released. Hesitantly, one by one, they sprang down from their cage onto the grass of the enclosure.

As the last young lion jumped down the huge male let out a roar. The crowd instinctively backed and the other animals stopped their striding, purring, chattering and snorting and stared, trying to fathom the intention behind the roar. There was no intention. Simla, the King of the Teerleber Lions, was nonplussed and, maybe, even a little afraid. Never before had he assembled his pride outside a cage and free. He just wanted to let off a little of his apprehension and assert his authority to tell all the other animals, and particularly his own pride, that he was still the king of all beasts.

For a moment no one moved. The roar of a lion is surely a terrible sound. It almost stops the blood circulating in the veins. The fat little Mayor Dowmen von Popolock, however, was in no way put out. He advanced to the cage of the Bengal tiger and calmly slid back the bolts. The excitement had grown to fever pitch. The roar of the lion had momentarily stopped many a human heartbeat and now the massive, much advertised and known to be ferocious king tiger was freed. Ladies fainted, children cried, strong men felt the terror of the moment. It was an awesome sight; the great tawny lions, clustered around the tiger cage, waiting his descent amongst them. Then the tiger sprang. 'Whoa!, ah!, ah!' sighed the crowd, their joint tension bursting out in one great expletive. Then a silence. It was as if everyone was holding their breath. Disbelief can be sent out into the ether just as can anger. Intangible, potent, wave after wave of it emanating from the turning upside down of lifelong and inherited acceptance of what should be. It was unbelievable, yet it was happening.

Oiler, the owl, had brought his wife and all his little

owlets. Mr Kämpfer was there in the neighbouring field, watching along with all the bulls and their cows. Neither animals nor humans had ever supposed they might see such a sight as was now on display before their very eyes.

The camels stared haughtily but safely as the great king tiger slowly passed them by with a grunt that sounded like good morning!

The powerful gorilla picked up a baby monkey and gently played with it like a father.

A goose ran between the vixen and her mate, who simply walked daintily by, followed by their cubs.

The lions strolled around the perimeter of the enclosure and laughed amongst themselves as the crowd – though thick steel bars separated them from the animals – moved back in natural fear.

'Anyone who cares to join me is welcome, shouted the Mayor. 'Come on. You, Mr Teerleber.'

The circus owner suddenly found himself walking away. He felt that he really should go and count the box office takings, which were so satisfactory.

'You, Dr Unterschnell,' but the good doctor suddenly thought of so many things he had left undone and which needed instant attention.

'Ah, well. You, Sir,' said the Mayor as he saw the famous Mr Leserschreibe. And so the crowd edged forward the reporter whose writings were so well known.

The King and Queen had come to see this unbelievable occurrence. Of course, they stood incognito among their people. Such a visit, with its pomp and show, would not have been allowed by the Waxindioren Parliament. It would be much too degrading for their Majesties to show interest in such activities. Yet it was just not to be missed. A once in a lifetime experience difficult for those who were not there to believe.

Sworn to secrecy, their personal servants had surrounded the royal couple as they left the palace and journeyed as commoners to the little town of Poppycock, with all its historic activities. The King had argued. He would not go. Yet he could not allow his Queen to go without him.

Standing watching, for the first time in her life among her subjects as one of them, the Queen heard her hero's invitation. She saw the reporter leave the enclosure unharmed. She heard the Mayor invite anyone to prove their courage. Before anyone could prevent it she stepped to the doorway of the enclosure and was welcomed in by the funny, fat, beaming Mayor of Poppycock whom she so admired.

Try to imagine it, all you who love the truths of yesteryear. Sixty-two animals, carnivore and herbivore, the powerful killers and the mild and gentle, all freely mixed together peacefully, enjoying each others' company and, in their midst, the fat, dumpy little man holding the hand of his yet unrecognised Queen. Never before had the King felt jealous but, as his Queen perambulated among the animals where he had not dared to go, he made a vow to rid the land of this clown of a Mayor. The Queen felt perfectly safe and marvelled at the Mayor's ability, for she heard him talking to the wild animals and it was obvious that they not only understood but replied.

'Careful,' said Popo. 'This lovely lady is your Queen.'

'Queen!' shrilled the big bull elephant. 'Did you all hear that? The Queen has come to see us.'

The animals clustered round. Of course, only Popo and they knew the great honour. Even the tiger came over and stood by the lady.

'May I roar?' asked the King lion. 'I don't want to frighten her, just to greet her properly.'

'You may all make your own greeting in a moment, when I give the signal,' said the Mayor. 'First I must prepare the Queen.'

'Your Majesty,' began Popo. 'The animals all wish to greet you in their own language. It will be a frightful noise but it is their way.'

'Sir Dowmen von Popo-lock,' said the Queen. 'They may certainly greet me as loudly as they will. I have no fear when you are here.'

So, unrecognised by the public and with her cloak hiding her true identity, the lady stood holding the hand of the funny, fat little Mayor of Poppycock while the spectators, all five thousand of them, witnessed the most spectacular, unbelievable and terrifying moments of their lives.

The sounds were hideous! It seemed neither lady nor fat little man could possibly survive but, in reality, what they unknowingly heard was the peaceful Animal Jubilation Greeting accorded only to royalty.

The Queen left the enclosure and, while all eyes were still fascinated by and focused on the group before them, joined her husband and retainers, who still remained unidentified among the crowds. They all watched until the lamps had to be lit and the animals returned to their cages.

Animals have short memories. They live for the day and carry over only general impressions. Some could not even remember the details of the previous day, but all were amazed to see and listen to the strange human who came each day to talk to them until they moved back to their duties in the circus. He saw to it that they had more food than ever before; he understood them and explained whatever they asked; he remained in their dreams all their lives, but never again did they mix, talk and learn about each other. And they failed utterly to make their grandchildren believe the happiness of that day.

The fame of the lordly Mayor Dowmen von Popo-lock spread far and wide and the little town of Poppycock became rich from tourists who, from that day to this, have visited to try to recapture some of the mystery for which the place is famous.